The Red Path, by Michael Wynn

	Page
Chapter 1: Roadblock	2
Chapter 2: Meeting	14
Chapter 3: Money Listens	29
Chapter 4: The Centre Cannot Hold	39
Chapter 5: Hills to Mills	50
Chapter 6 Tanks to Transit	71
Chapter 7: Banks Not Made of Marble	83
Chapter 8: Oil for Peace	97
Chapter 9: Canada, Reconstituted	108
Chapter 10: Food, Clothing, and Shelter	126
Chapter 11: The Land	135
Ten Years Later	144
Fifty Years Later	145
About the author	147

Chapter 1: Roadblock

"Where's the key, Sarah?"

"I'll tell you when the trucks get off my land."

Sarah David, 93, gazed up at the Royal Canadian Mounted Police (RCMP) officer.

"Where's the key, Sarah?"

The officer's dark face scowled, but he held his temper. He was surrounded by cell phones, ready to photograph his every move.

"You heard me. Move the trucks and I'll tell you where the key is." Sarah rattled the chain that locked her wheelchair tightly to the rack of propane tanks that lay across the narrow road.

It seems that he hadn't heard Sarah the first time, but the RCMP was historically deaf to Indians. Even Indigenous RCMP cultivated a deafness to their own people. Some would retire early to lives driven by social work to make up for years of arresting their own people.

It is like the judge who, asked to reflect on his years on the bench, said, "Well, I freed some people who were guilty and I jailed some people who were innocent, so on average, justice was done."

Average justice, like depending on the doctor who got 51% in medical school to operate on your tubal pregnancy. More than one Cariboo women never woke up from what should be a routine operation, but in the British Columbia Cariboo, the only routine for generations was injustice. Injustice from the land-thieving settlers, injustice incited among the Indians.

The RCMP presided over this toxic situation, but an air of purity was blowing in the Cariboo, and blowing out the rot. Move with the breeze or be blown away by it.

The force was an 1870s colonial concoction to keep Indians off land recently stolen from them. Now history moved in a direction that neither the RCMP, nor its government masters, nor its government's corporate masters, controlled.

The officer spun on heel, a grouchy pirouette, and retreated to the nervous men clustered around the police cars.

"Well, Officer Boucher?" a grey-haired man asked. The man below the hair was Simon van der Waals, a mining engineer who parlayed that expertise into a mining fortune. For the first time since Honduras, van der Waals was nervous. His fortune cookie seemed to be crumbling.

"Sarah won't move until your trucks get out," Officer Boucher explained.

A younger man, more nervous than van der Waals, whispered in his ear, "Sir, we must break ground today, before the stock market closes, or Dream Metals is in trouble."

"I know that, Mike. I didn't make a mining fortune ignoring the stock market."

Mike Vidic kicked the dust with his expensive shoe. If Dream Metals was in trouble, he was out of a job. His financial wizardry seemed no match for an old woman on a bush road. If only those cell phone people would bug off. A welder could cut the chain, careful not to spark the tanks and blow up everyone. They could break ground in time for the shareholders to see it via satellite and keep the share price from plummeting. Dream Metals plummets. Mike Vidic plummets.

Van der Waals turned to the RCMP, as corporate people have for generations, mostly in Canada but more recently also in other countries which needed a police state for profits.

"Officer, you must get that woman off the road. These trucks must get to the site and break ground. We need to upload photos to investors, or tomorrow there will be no Dream Metals Corporation, no mine, and there might be more chaos than you or I can predict."

"I'm doing my best, sir. We dare not cut the chain in this heat, with those propane tanks so close."

"I know. May I talk to her?"

"Be my guest."

Van der Waals walked up to Sarah David. Their eyes met. They understood each other, and they understood that today one would lose, one would win.

"Thanks for coming to see me, Mr. van der Waals," Sarah cheerily said. "I'm happy to meet you."

"I respect you, Mrs. David, but this has gone on long enough," van der Waals said. "People could get hurt. You could get hurt."

"I'm an old woman. I have been hurt before, for less reason than this. Please take your trucks off our land. Dig for minerals on other land."

"Yes, we can dig elsewhere, but if we don't dig here, then our company might die. You wouldn't want hundreds of people to lose their jobs, would you?"

"If you dig here, then our land will die, our water, our animals, our way of life will die," Sarah said. "We have tried to stop you with talk, with scientists, and in court. We will stop you here."

"'We' who, Mrs. David? I see only you here."

"Others are with me. One of them has the key to this lock," she replied.

"Where is the key?"

"I'll tell you when your trucks leave."

"I don't want to hurt you."

"I'm an old lady. I have been hurt for worse reasons than defending my land." Sarah winked at the cell phone cameras trained on the two of them.

Van der Waals saw the wink, and smiled. "I admire you."

"Why?"

"You stand up for your land. Long ago, my people stood up for their land in South Africa. The English attacked them and took the land."

"Sounds familiar," Sarah said. "The English took our land, and killed many who defended it."

"There must be a better way, a peaceful way," van der Waals sighed. He glanced at his watch. The stock market closed in less than an hour. He heard Mike Vidic's shoes scuff in the dust behind him. Why do I hire such callous people, he wondered. Force didn't work in Honduras, even with the RCMP and the Canadian Army trying to help keep that mine open. People poured in, took over, cameras recorded it, the government threw Dream Metals out of the country, and the stock market noticed. Blasted stock market. Capitalism needs re-engineering.

"There must be a better way," he repeated.

"There is," Sarah said. "Get your trucks off our land, and let's talk."

Did she know that if the trucks left now, that people in distant Vancouver and New York would devalue Dream Metals shares enough to bankrupt the company?

"I know your company is in trouble," Sarah added, seeming to read van der Waals' mind.

Who was this woman? How did she know?

"At our general band meeting the other day, we heard about the trouble that Dream Metals is in. That's one reason that I'm here today."

"You want to drive Dream Metals out of business?" Vander Waals asked incredulously.

"Yes."

"Why, for goodness sake?"

"You said there must be a better way. We found one."

"How will killing Dream Metals help you defend your land? Other mining companies might come."

"We doubt it. After what we put you through, no other mining companies will dare to come."

Van der Waals laughed out loud. "I like you. You're tough, like me."

"I'm a Chilcotin elder. I didn't get old being weak, but you're not enough like me. I can help you be more like me," she said, again that twinkling eye.

Sarah David and Simon van der Waals smiled at each other. There was a long silence.

Dream Metals Chief Financial Officer Mike Vidic's pricy feet scuffled. RCMP Officer David Boucher fidgeted. Crows cawed overhead.

Boucher didn't ask for this when he joined the RCMP back in Quebec. He was the pride of his Naskapi people, acting for justice when they so needed it. He had helped jail a thieving chief before he joined up. His granny was so proud of him. She was proud, but not as proud, when he said he'd go to Regina to join the RCMP. The conversation replayed in his mind as if it was yesterday, not three years ago.

"Don't join the police, David," she said. "They haven't done much for us, especially the Surete du Quebec. Remember when they killed your cousin Arthur in the cell in Sept Iles?"

"I remember, Granny, but this is the RCMP, not the Surete. These are the good cops. Remember when I took you to Rimouski to watch their musical ride?"

"They do more than ride. They're cops. They ride on us. Don't join. You might be arresting your own people."

"I would never arrest my own people. Besides, here it's Surete, not RCMP. I'll be out west, ticketing speeders, arresting drug dealers, stopping thieves like our ex-chief."

"I can't stop you, but I can tell you that you won't like it," were her last words on the subject.

Now here I am, trying to arrest someone who reminds me of my grandmother, Boucher thought. Granny was right. Is this old woman in the wheelchair right?

Van der Waals walked back to Boucher and Vidic. "We're gonna talk tomorrow, her people and I."

"Tomorrow will be too late for Dream Metals," Vidic protested.

"We will find a better way," Van der Waals explained.

Vidic hated when his boss got mystical. Mysticism has no place in business. Business is about numbers, investment, risk, share value, and above all, profit. No profit, no business. No business, no future for Canada or the world. I didn't claw my way out of the Eastside of Vancouver and through business school to die of mysticism, Vidic thought. I paid my way through university by doing mining jobs in the summer. Apartheid South Africa paid his way through engineering. When the blacks took over South Africa, he fled to Canada. The Indians aren't about to take over Canada.

I remember my roots. My dad fought to free Croatia from Yugoslavia. He did some mean but necessary things. When we fled to Canada, he didn't tell the immigration people half of what he did back in Croatia. He did what was necessary. Why won't van der Waals?

Van der Waals forgets his roots, Vidic thought. If this company crashes, I'll happily work for someone who believes in business, not mysticism. The tough survive, in Croatia and in Canada.

Mike Vidic had yet to imagine working for himself, by working with others, not against them, not for the rich who could discard him like the Croat rich discarded his father.

"Let's go," Vander Waals said.

Vidic sighed in frustration. Boucher sighed in relief.

My company is no more, van der Waals thought, more wistful than sad. All I worked for in Canada, all I dreamed in South Africa, will evaporate with morning trading in the stock market.

I would have been happy to stay in South Africa after the blacks took over. They needed mining engineers, but dad insisted that I take Johanna and their daughter Maria out of the country. Johanna's psychology training and experience quickly landed her a job in Vancouver.

Johanna's ancestors had been in an English prison camp during the Boer War in 1899. She was more nervous than he was about the future of South Africa. Canada gave them a nice life. A life of her dreams? Of his? A nightmare for Canada's Indians, as life under English oppression had been for Johanna's ancestors.

South Africa learned apartheid well from Canada, but apartheid was finished there. Soon finished in Canada too?

Dad sneered that South Africa would decline under "those blacks." Dad was a young Boer policeman in Sharpeville in 1960. Our circumstances shape us, van der Waals thought. What will shape me here? What will old Sarah David tell me tomorrow?

Perhaps these people need an engineer, van der Waals hoped.

A dusty rumble of trucks carefully turned around, recorded by cell phones and a couple shoulder-mounted movie cameras. The people were too nervous to rejoice.

The RCMP packed up, started cruisers, and turned around. A few cheers went up.

Boucher's heart sank. His grandmother was right.

Van der Waals drove his jeep, Vidic frowning beside him.

"I don't blame you, Mike," van der Waals said. "This was a long time coming. It didn't start here."

"Dream Metals is in trouble, Simon," Vidic offered. "What will we do?"

"Mike, you're a smart guy. You'll survive. The world will always need good planners and number crunchers."

"It's as if I let you down, Simon."

"You didn't, Mike. Nobody could have predicted Honduras, and now Fish Lake resistance. You and I were born in countries where unpredictable things happened. We lived through that. Now Canada seems unpredictable. We'll live through this."

Mike Vidic's frown turned to puzzlement. "Mr. Vander Waals, you lost your company, but I only lost my job. Why are you more cheerful than I am?"

"Mike, I'm 62, a millionaire, and I made my fortune in Canada. My dad was a policeman, my mom a bookkeeper for an insurance company. Living under apartheid benefitted us, got me into university, and helped get me into Canada; but richer whites than us gained much more from apartheid. Your family came from a country acutely torn by class divisions, Mike. That's one reason I hired you."

"I don't understand."

"Your parents grew up in Tito's Yugoslavia, and you were a teenager when your country fell apart. Tito didn't solve class divisions any better than Vorster did in South Africa, but your mother went to university. Her peasant parents didn't predict that, but they fought alongside Tito's partisans against the Nazis and Ustasha. They fought for a country in which their smart daughter could leave the farm and go to medical school. I remember your parents."

"My parents were on opposite sides of a war that ended my chances of going to university," Vidic said. "They divorced soon after we came to Canada." Vidic was amazed that van der Waals remembered so many details from his life. It seemed that he was listening, even when Vidic thought he wasn't.

"Your dad, like my dad, did what he thought was necessary at the time. They were survivors, adapters. We will survive and adapt, Mike."

"My dad saved us from Serbian brutes," Vidic said. "He got us out of there just in time. My mother was far away in Belgrade at some clinic."

"Your mother was trying to keep the country together, in her way," van der Waals said. "Her clinic treated anyone who walked in, any wounded, no questions asked."

A tear came to Vidic's eyes as he remembered the night his father came, bleeding, to their tiny Belgrade apartment. Mother kept some medical supplies at home, a habit from her partisan parents: battlefield medicine. She took out the shell fragments and sewed his wounded thigh and shoulder. Then they talked all night.

Vidic was 14. He wanted to go with his dad to fight in Croatia, but his parents had different plans for him.

"We're going to Canada," Mother said, with a finality that even his father didn't oppose.

"I want to fight for my country," Vidic boasted, unaware that it was disappearing under his feet.

"Mother is right, Mikhail. We must leave. If we stay, and my enemies find and kill me, they'll probably kill you as well. Don't ask what I did in Krajina."

Mother's face looked very old at that moment, as if a dream had died within her.

A year later in Vancouver, Vidic's anger exploded into lumpen violence among gangsters he admired. Father called them cowardly children, to their faces. They never challenged him, but they made Vidic earn a place among them by stealing cars, and worse.

Mike Vidic ran wild while Mother was at the University of British Columbia qualifying to be a doctor in Canada. Father went from job to job before Croat contacts took him under their wing and into their construction company. Mother never trusted these people who came to Canada to avoid living in Tito's Yugoslavia.

Father never hit her. One day they argued in Serbo-Croat, their language of argument. They argued like two intellectuals, not like the swinish rabble in their Eastside neighborhood. The next day Father was gone.

The next day Mikhail Vidic was in court for breaking and entering. His friends had fled and left him by the broken window on Howe Street. Who'd break into a mining company office?

That's the day Mike Vidic met Simon van der Waals, the owner of that mining company.

Van der Waals and his lawyer talked excitedly while the judge droned on about wayward youth, Young Offenders' Act leniency, the fiasco of sentencing circles, the need to set an example, the day's heavy case load.

"Mike Vidic, I find you guilty of breaking and entering," the judge pontificated. "Would you like to say anything before I sentence you?"

"No, sir."

"I would like to say something," van der Waals' lawyer interjected.

He probably wants a tougher sentence, Vidic thought. I wish I could afford a fancy lawyer.

"My client sees no gain in jailing this young man. He proposes community service."

The judge sighed. "What service does he have in mind?"

Van der Waals rose. "I want this young man to go with me to a charitable agency my spouse runs. He will work there for three months, pay his debt to me and to society, and perhaps turn his life around."

"Counsel for the defense, do you agree?" the judge asked Vidic's harried young lawyer.

"Yes, your honor."

"I thereby release Mike Vidic on the recognizance of Simon van der Waals," the judge ruled.

"Vidic must see a probation officer twice per month for six months. Failure to meet this requirement will land him back in this court, and probably in young offender detention."

Vidic eyed van der Waals as the court guard led him to the older, blond man. "Am I to be his grateful slave now?" he thought.

"Young man, I want you to come with me," Simon said.

"Yes, sir," Mike replied.

"I don't know you, but I want to do something for you. Something in the way you carry yourself tells me that you can be more than a petty gangster."

The two left the courtroom and strode into a drizzly Vancouver November. A jeep pulled up. They got into the back seat.

"Where to, Simon?" the driver asked.

"Thanks for picking us up, Patrice. We'll go to Lost and Found Innocents. I have a surprise for Johanna."

As Patrice manoeuvred the jeep east on Georgia Street, he wondered about the surprise, but he didn't wonder much. Van der Waals was full of surprises. The first surprise was hiring Patrice, a Congolese refugee. This was an unusual South African indeed.

On a street off East Hastings, the jeep stopped in front of an old but well-kept brick building.

Vidic realized they were in his neighborhood, but he didn't recognize the building. Before he could worry about what slavery the court had imposed on him, a matronly woman came down the sidewalk and hugged Simon as he got out of the jeep.

"Thanks, Patrice, for delivering my husband again. Could you come back in three hours?"

"Yes, Johanna. Do you need anything?"

"Patrice, could you find these things," Johanna said, handing him a list. "Use your purchase order book if you can't charge them to our account."

Organized woman, this one, Patrice thought. Her ancestors conquered the Zulu with guns, but she conquered me with trust. Who else would trust a refugee with a book of signed purchase orders? Patrice noticed that most of the list was office supplies, with a few food items and toys thrown in.

Perhaps he'd stop at home and bring Franz along for the ride. It was his brother's day off. He was still at that Burnaby warehouse that hired them both when they arrived from Congo.

Franz was a foreman now, and he treated new immigrants better than foremen had treated him. They'd find this stuff and get back by 2:00 easily. The van der Waals didn't mind Franz going along for the ride. Patrice repaid their trust with honesty.

Patrice was named after Patrice Lumumba, the legendary Congolese leader. His brother Franz was named after the Martinique-born psychiatrist Franz Fanon, who helped the Algerians throw out the French. Fanon didn't live to see a free Algeria, but his namesake vowed to see a Congo free of meddling and oppression by foreigners and their comprador collaborators. The brothers were only refugees until their country was safe to return to, that is, when it was again their country.

Vidic watched the jeep drive away. Simon and Johanna watched Vidic.

"Johanna, I brought that help we discussed," Simon said. "You told me that things have piled up since the Haitians came. This resourceful young man will help."

"Another young offender, Simon?" Johanna asked.

"Yep."

"Childsafe?"

"Yep."

"For how long this time?"

"Three months."

Johanna paused and pondered. "I'll keep him plenty busy." She turned to Vidic. "My name is Johanna van der Waals. What's yours?"

"Mike Vidic," he answered, expecting an interrogation.

"What you did to land here is none of my business. What you do here is my business," Mike.

"Call me Johanna."

No interrogation.

Simon trailed behind as Mike and Johanna went through the front door, serious steel. They took off their wet shoes and coats in the entry way. As Mike hung his coat, he noticed several other coats, including small children's coats on a lower rack. He heard children's voices down the hall. A day care? But these voices did not sound like those of children at play.

A large bright room greeted the trio. A toddler in dreadlocks ran up and hugged Johanna. She
held a ragdoll in one hand. "Marie is happy to see you, Johanna," she squeaked.

"I'm happy to see Marie, and you Pauline," Johanna said, crouching down to look at Pauline.

Johanna rose and addressed the 10-odd children and two young woman in the room, "Simon has brought someone to help us for three months, everyone."

The two young women's faces brightened. One said, "And we sure need the help, Simon," before the two returned their attention to the children.

Mike looked at the women, at the children, and thought that this was no day care, even though it looked like one. The children seemed hardened, edgy, too eager to please. Where had he seen children like this before? Back in Croatia during the war.

"Mike," Johanna said. "Simon told me that you survived the war in Croatia. When he said that, I knew that you were the man for the job here at Lost and Found Innocents. Each of these children survived war, too."

"I started this charity soon after we came from South Africa to Canada. I was working as a hospital psychologist and seeing many refugees traumatized by war. My acute care hospital duties left me little time to do anything for them, so I started Lost and Found Innocents."

"A grant from the hospital foundation helped. We converted this abandoned sweatshop into what you see today. The bankrupt owner was happy to part with it. My financial wizard husband helped organize the financing, but now most of our money comes from the refugee community."

"As you can see, Mike," we are three women running this. Filsan is from Somalia. Harbinder is from Punjab. They came to Canada as refugees, as you did. Our building is old, like the maintenance man who volunteers his time; but there are things he needs help doing. That's where you come in. Welcome."

Vidic thought, if puttering around here for three months keeps me out of jail, fine with me.

"I know a few things about maintenance, from working with my dad at his company."

"Good," Johanna said. "How are you with numbers?"

Vidic remembered how easy math had been for him in Burnaby North Secondary School that first year in Canada. English had been a harder challenge.

"Pretty good."

"That might be handy," she said. "So you're all set, Mike. Randy our maintenance man should be here in a few minutes. He usually starts at 11:00. Patrice will drive you home at two o'clock."   She turned to Simon, who was heading for his coat and shoes. See you tonight.

"Bye," Simon said. "I'll catch the Skytrain back downtown."

That day, Mike fixed the bathroom door lock, unplugged a toilet, raked the lawn, and met Frank, the maintenance man. Frank had worked all over British Columbia and was now retired. He knew a lot about building maintenance, but he was no longer able to do some things. He would explain them to Mike, who would do them.

The two got on well. This would be easier than stealing for gangs.

By the time Patrice picked up Mike at 2:00 to drive him home, Mike had good news for his mother, for a change.

"Do you want to come with me to Nemiah tomorrow, Mike?" Simon asked, as he steered the jeep over the Chilcotin River Bridge at Stone.

How could Mike refuse this man, whose wife's funky charity got him out of gangs and on the track to business school? He found the Simon Fraser University math more challenging than Burnaby North Secondary math had been, but he quickly caught on. Studying finance really inspired him: money was the blood of society, especially capitalist society. Mike could almost hear money flowing out of his credit union account, as blood had flown out of father that night in Belgrade. Blood and money. Blood money?

"Sure, I'll go. It's not as if I have a job as of tomorrow, when the stock market kills Dream Metals."

"We are survivors, Mike, like the kids in Lost and Found Innocents. We'll survive this. We might emerge happier for it. Who knows?"

Who knows, Mike thought, as the jeep turned onto Highway 20 toward Williams Lake.

Chapter 2: Meeting

The rosy-fingered dawn lay across Konni Lake as Sarah David stoked the fire in the wood stove that heated her log house. Her grandson Randy had started the fire last night before he went to bed. The chill fall air comes soon to the Snow Mountains. It was late September. "Randy is so good to me," thought Sarah. "I think I'll make him a new pair of gloves."

There was a knock at the door.

"Are you up, Sarah?" Chief Marnie Triste asked, in her sad but sing-song voice.

"Come in, dear," Sarah said, as she put the kettle on the stove and walked across the room to get the bannock and jam.

"I brought some wild potatoes," Marnie said as she came in. "I was going to bring dry meat, but the moose that I shot two days ago is still hanging in pieces in my shed," Marnie continued apologetically. "I've been so busy."

"Thanks for the spuds, Marnie," Sarah said. "Don't worry about the moose. I'll help you with it after today's meeting with the mining people. We all have a lot to do lately, but I think we'll look back later and be glad we were so busy with these things. I'm old and won't see much of the new world we're bringing, but you're young and you'll see it. My grandson Randy will see it. His children will see it. Many Chilcotins will see it."

"You were brave on the roadblock yesterday, Sarah," Marnie said. "I have a good feeling about today."

"I have a good feeling about you, Marnie," Sarah said. "You have been brave, standing up for us against the mine and the government. My grandma would have been proud."

Marnie blushed. Grandma David was a legend among the Chilcotin. She was one of two little girls who survived when smallpox killed hundreds at Puntzi in 1864. She came to Nemiah Valley soon after, as many Chilcotin survivors did. This remote area protected them from smallpox and other settler schemes to kill Chilcotins and steal their land. Now they had their land back more firmly than any Canadian court would ever allow. Chilcotin traditional law would rule again, as it had not since settler trickery overturned it in the 1860s.

Now they needed to stand together to defend that law and land, again; and they needed help. Would these two mining men help?

Marnie Triste need not be sad or apologetic, because while her people slept after yesterday's confrontation, that confrontation rallied support near and far. Help was coming on a bigger scale and from stranger sources than she imagined.

Cariboo activists, indigenous and settler, whose cell phones had recorded yesterday's roadblock victory over the miners, had uploaded their images worldwide. People from many places in Canada and the United States were on their way to Nemiah. Others had gathered the courage to confront corporate schemers in Canada and beyond its borders. Still more were sending money and messages of solidarity.

Even Dream Metals was helping the Chilcotin, and not only by dying on the trading floor of stock markets in Vancouver and New York. Two major Canadian banks would probably go down with the company, their bonds worthless paper now, their other natural resource stocks declining in value as people rose against mines, pipelines, and logging in Canada and beyond. Long-simmering resentment of the banks by an increasing number of their victims had spawned a movement to nationalize the banks. The army was in a foreign quagmire defending resource operations such as Dream Metals had, operations now under such threat that the government refused to bring enough army home to attack the Chilcotins and others who seized this chance to make a government for all, not just for the rich.

One old woman on a roadblock was the spark that ignited a political fire whose future none could predict, but whose future all could control.

As the teapot sang in boil, Marnie reached for another bannock. Sarah's house always relaxed her, recharged her to return to the settler world to fight for her people, to fight for Sarah.

Even Mike Vidic was relaxed, as he drove for his boss, or was Simon Vander Waals his ex-boss now that Dream Metals was no more? Mike did not feel as if he had lost anything. IT was as if he was embarking on an adventure more interesting than the one that had brought his parents and him from war-ravaged Yugoslavia to Canada almost 20 years earlier. That country's recent reunification was news that almost made him want to venture back there.

Simon van der Waals, in the passenger seat, alternately gazed out the window and wrote on a pad of paper on his lap. Like Mike, he was eager for this adventure.

Many vehicles had passed them on Highway 20 from Williams Lake to Lee's Corner, the turnoff to Nemiah. The Lookout a few kilometres before the turnoff had been full of vehicles, people milling around, even horses nibbling on the roadside grass. Dust that hung in the air on the Nemiah road told both men that there were vehicles ahead of them.

This would be no ordinary meeting.

"I'm glad you came along, Mike," Simon said. "I think you'll be very helpful."

Some days, Mike couldn't fathom how Simon had such faith in him, a Vancouver street thug who blossomed into a financier under this South African immigrant engineer.

"I'm curious to see what's next," Mike said, an understatement each man felt with some fear but more excitement.

They crossed the Taseko River Bridge. The river was low. Winter was coming. Some morning mist swirled above the burbling aquamarine water. Vehicles, people, and horses crowded the riverside parking lot. So many people. What were they thinking?

Now they were in the Brittany Triangle, real Indian country, and how, since yesterday. "The king's writ doesn't rule here anymore," Mike thought, remembering his Tito partisan grandfather's line about the exiled king of Yugoslavia. "Perhaps we'll get the People's Republic right this time," he pondered.

"It's as if we're entering another country," Simon said, seeming to read Mike's mind. "I hope we're as welcome today as we were yesterday after the roadblock."

"I hope they need us," Mike continued the train of thought. "We sure need them now."

"'Us' and 'Them' has been the problem for centuries," Simon said. "I believe there's a way to make all of us 'We.'"

Spoken like a man who didn't live through a civil war, Mike thought, but he shared Simon's hope.

The Naughtaneqed School gym was packed, more than for any funeral, the usual reason for a full gym. Life and the future, not death and the past, had filled it. Many stood around outside, talking and joking. Many did likewise inside.

The oral tradition.

"Well, Holly, no mining job for you, eh?" old Rodney Iqallie joked to the young woman standing beside him outside the gym. The glowing fall morning sun makes autumn special in Nemiah, and anywhere that people still respect the sun, water, land, and one another.

"Old man, now you'll have to support me," Holly Daniels joked.

"You probably can't even cook. Did they teach you that in trucking school?" Rodney joked back. "I need a traditional woman, who'll skin my moose and warm my bed."

"I'd skin you in your bed, Rodney. Your bone is probably more like moose nose and less like moose bone at your age. Your years of warming up women are over."

"Hey, respect your elders, young lady," Rodney said. He looked around. "There sure are lots of strangers here today. Big meeting, I guess. That Sarah David, as tough as her grandmother."

Matrilineal society hadn't died. It had just hidden from the settlers for a few generations. Sarah David. Holly Daniels. Decades separated them in age, but traditions united them in wisdom. And today's meeting needed wisdom.

Inside the gym, Sarah David talked to a couple band councillors while Marnie Triste hooked up and tested the microphones at the front, sides, and back of the gym. Everybody could have a say today. We need all the ideas we can get. Marnie's sad eyes didn't look so sad today. "Triste" means "sad" in French. The Oblate Catholic priests came from France on heels of the British Army in the 1870s, stuck French names to her ancestors, and carted the children off to the residential school near Williams Lake.

"Did the Oblates see my ancestors as sad?" Marnie wondered. "I'm sure glad they left our area and only have a handful of priests marauding around Canada now."

There were no more Oblates in Northern Quebec, for example. David Boucher, fresh out of Regina and posted in his Naskapi homeland, had arrested the last one for child abuse.

Boucher wasn't thinking about Oblates as he drove his RCMP truck across the Taseko River Bridge, however; but he was wondering about his Naskapi homeland. Last night's phone call from his cousin in Natashquan had riled him up at first, but given him ideas.

His people, and other indigenous people in Quebec, and many settlers, had taken the law into their own hands. The police officer in him rebelled at this. The Naskapi in him rejoiced when he heard the story.

The Quebec government's "Plan Nord" was over, thanks to resentment that had built for months across the province. Resentment was acute among his people, who were tired of seeing their forests clear-cut, their minerals dug up, their rivers dammed or polluted, or both, none of it any benefit to them.

Great Whale River people had started it by seizing the local Hydro Quebec generating station. Before the Surete du Quebec could dispatch enough police officers to retake the station, occupations and seizures sprang up in lumber and paper mills, mines, and even a couple ports on the Lower North Shore of the St. Lawrence River. Demonstrations against "Plan Nord" had been growing larger all summer in Quebec City and Montreal. Neither rural nor urban dwellers were benefiting from this fire sale of Quebec natural resources to foreign and domestic companies.

There were not enough police to go round. Many chose not to go anywhere. Valcartier army base did not have enough soldiers to restore order. Ottawa had seen to that when it sent most of them to Congo to help quell an uprising against foreign mining companies, many of them Canadian.

The federal government feared that Valcartier soldiers could not be depended on to keep order in Quebec. The few who remained at the base confirmed Ottawa's suspicions by refusing to help the Montreal police quash the growing demonstrations.

Even the Montreal police were only half-hearted in their efforts. Now the Surete were overstretched and rapidly losing interest in sacrificing themselves for businesses and their government friends.

Today there would be a mass meeting in the Paul Sauve Arena in Quebec City, and another in Olympic Stadium in Montreal. By the time David Boucher finished his RCMP shift, Quebec and even Canada might be very different from what they were this crisp autumn morning.

As Boucher parked his RCMP truck, he saw a crowd gather, away from the door to the gym. Boucher felt more relaxed, more welcome than he had felt at yesterday's roadblock.

"Albert, we gotta get in there and be heard."

"Bruce, every time you come here, it's trouble. Let us do it our own Chilcotin way."

"I agree, Albert. I just wanna offer helpful legal advice. I got those Oka guys out of jail on appeal, didn't I?"

"Yeah. Let's go in. But don't take over the floor."

"I couldn't if I wanted to, Albert. This is bigger than me, bigger than you, bigger than everything that has happened in this country since Europeans washed up on its shores."

"You're European, Bruce. Remember that. No high words. Explain your legal bafflegab better this time."

"Easy, Albert. He's on our side," an man older than Albert told Albert. Why did an old man, who didn't know law from ladders, trust this lawyer more than Albert did, Boucher wondered. Daniels didn't know much law, but he had a degree, albeit in social work.

Social work had radicalized more people than he could remember, Boucher thought. Perhaps some social workers tired of treating poverty, addiction, family violence, and crime without addressing their underlying economic and racist causes.

Quebec cops seemed tired of bashing heads for the rich. Boucher was tired of arresting drunk drivers and petty thieves while ignoring the reasons they drink and steal. Was he becoming a radical cop, like the cops in Quebec?

Boucher watched this animated conversation from the edge of the crowd it had drawn. The crowd included Chilcotins and non-Chilcotins, some he knew from past activist escapades, some he didn't know. The crowd entered the hall as one.

Albert Daniels and Bruce Culloden were strange bedfellows, Boucher thought as he followed the crowd into the packed gym. Last year, Albert practically ran the lawyer out of Nemiah for opposing the band's decision to block the road to Fish Lake. Culloden had been right to oppose the decision, though, with injunctions about to bankrupt the band. Culloden had gone to provincial court in Williams Lake to overturn the injunctions and he had succeeded.

Culloden succeeded against the injunctions partly due to an earlier, partial victory in the Supreme Court of Canada: Chilcotins had traditional use rights to their land, but not outright title. This opaque Canadian compromise offended few and pleased few. Indians seeking justice in Canadian courts was like hosts seeking justice from parasites, Albert had thought during the land claim's long and expensive rise through the court system.

The Supreme Court ruling had helped Culloden back in Williams Lake court, though. The local judge, a good old boy who wore cowboy boots more firmly than he wore justice, had been averse to putting the Chilcotins on a long road of appeal, this time likely a shorter road than the road to the Supreme Court had been.

Provincial Court Judge Clarence "Click" Helmcken proudly traced his ancestors to one of those Englishmen who spread smallpox among the Chilcotins to "pre-empt" their land in the 1860s. A Quesnel lawyer had trolled archives to prove the attempted genocide. A retired school principal's history columns in the local newspapers ignored the attempt and glorified the pre-empt. Men who purposely infected Chilcotins with smallpox became sturdy pioneers in the retired principal's pungent prose. What becomes history depends on who writes history.

Judge Helmcken, "Click" his somewhat-mocking nickname from his frequently-misfiring gun at turkey shoots, was a hometown boy from Clinton, in the Cariboo. He proudly boasted his village's 1863 pioneer beginnings, but didn't mention that Indians were dying all around in the 1860s to enable this pioneering.

He who controls the present controls the past. He who controls the past controls the future, English iconoclastic writer George Orwell wrote. Now, different people, more people, the people, were taking control of the present. Raise a roadblock to stop a mine. Raise public consciousness to remove roadblocks to education, roadblocks of the mind, roadblocks of nonsense by retired principals, roadblocks of cowboy bluster by judges.

Chilcotins had inconveniently survived attempted genocide by smallpox, and genocide by residential schools. Too much residential school legacy had slithered into the public schools that continued to under-educate Indians. The residential schools had self- destructed in the puff of smoke from fiery scandals of sex abuse, racism, and worse.

More indigenous children languished in non-indigenous foster care than suffered in the residential schools at their height, Albert Daniels well knew. That was changing thanks to indigenous social service agencies, but a government stick still herded those agencies. A government carrot of money tantalized and controlled even indigenous agencies, compromising the care of their children. Albert Daniels was tired of compromise, and he wasn't alone. Albert had recommend hiring Culloden, another person of strong opinions, but ones in accord with Chilcotin ways. Culloden seemed able to get the stick out of the government's hands. What else could he do with this settler justice system. What could he do to this settler justice, mostly injustice? Could he help replace it? Much was possible now that had had been unthinkable mere months ago.

Helmcken spied possibilities for himself, political possibilities. He would like to parlay his bench renown into a seat in the provincial legislature, perhaps even the federal parliament. He saw the 25% of the population that was indigenous as potential voters. Luckily, Canada's lurches toward United States hyper democracy, driven by the rhetoric of freedom but fertilized by lobbyists and money, did not include voting for judges. Culloden remember his canny father's phrase, "In the United Snakes, they even vote for the dogcatcher."

"Click" Helmcken had mis-engaged his political and legal brains before shooting off his settler mouth. He had overturned the injunction against the Fish Lake road blockade. What a bonus to the Chilcotins, perhaps more than "Click" intended. Useful idiot.

Helmcken was fresh from explaining, more explaining away, that racist poster found on his website, that poster of a shooting range target painted on an Indian. That racist joke from a Kootenay Royal Canadian Legion joke had gone viral, like smallpox.

Culloden's dad, a war veteran, was turning in his grave over that poster. The Legion, now bursting with reactionary veterans of Canada's illegal foreign wars in Haiti, Bosnia, Africa, and elsewhere, wasn't the place of peace education that it had been for his dad's World War Two comrades.

Settler justice, wearing its blindfold in that famous statue outside the Supreme Court building in Ottawa, was reputedly blind, that is, impartial. This system, fixed onto Indians like a legal hair shirt by those who stole Indian land, wasn't impartial. Culloden had argued that in law journals, even mainstream law journals, even international law journals. In Williams Lake, justice had usually also been deaf to Indians, until Helmcken's welcome and helpful ruling in the

Chilcotins' favor. Exasperated Chilcotins welcomed the refund of the fines they had incurred for violating the injunction. Good riddance to a bad injunction.

Bruce Culloden had caused trouble that day last year by opposing the roadblock until he could defeat the injunction that threatened to bankrupt the Chilcotins, and even jail some of them, perhaps Albert, perhaps Bruce. Albert Daniels was slow to admit he was wrong, but his grudging friendliness with Bruce implied that he trusted the lawyer. Albert trusted few lawyers. It seemed that the two men were reconciled.

Tremble, miners, Boucher thought: courage plus legality might equal victory.

Tremble, Officer David, Boucher thought: oppose my RCMP bosses and confirm their suspicions that I'm an "Indian lover," and lose my job in the bargain.

Regina didn't train me for this, Boucher thought. His grandmother's wisdom would be more useful here today. What is it about grandmothers, anyway?

"Good morning, everyone. Thanks for coming," Chief Marnie said into the microphone, her voice echoing around the hall, and reaching outside thanks to the speakers mounted outside the gym.

"We have finally convinced the miners not to dig up our land and lake and wreck our water. Yesterday was quite a day, eh?"

A boisterous cheer went up, and included a couple war whoops from men and women, some young, some not so young. People were full of energy today.

"Now what do we do?" she asked. "We have support from all over the Chilcotin, from Canada, and even from other countries. On behalf of our people, I welcome our visitors today. Thanks for coming to our land and standing by us."

"Our action yesterday inspired people all over Canada. Some blocked rail lines. Some blocked highways. Some occupied government offices. Some occupied band offices."

"We didn't occupy our band office, Marnie. You're doing good," someone wisecracked from the crowd, which laughed.

"Hey, thanks, but this is a stressful job. You want it? You can have it! Put your smart mouth to work for all of us," she replied. Again the crowd laughed.

Clever politician, Simon van der Waals thought from his seat near the back of the gym. More like her in South Africa and it wouldn't have been such a violent fiasco, first ending apartheid, then ending the African National Congress policies that kept inequality entrenched. A truly socialist South Africa sure shook up, and shook off, the international mining industry. The country was now a model of democracy, true economic democracy. The people who worked in the mines shared the mines' bounty, with plenty left for the public purse.

If Canada was going that way, Simon hoped it would be a less-violent transition than South Africa had endured. Perhaps these friendly Canadians would stay friendly, bundle up together in their frosty climate, not battle in their cities, nor in their mines.

"Tea, Simon?" Mike asked, offering a cup.

"Thanks, Mike."

Marnie was talking about Quebec, now. This was news to most of the crowd, if not to Boucher.

"The police are trained to use violence to keep us down, but they can use it to defend us, too," she said. "In Quebec, they're siding with the Indians, today, right now. They refuse to arrest people for roadblocks, occupations, demonstrations. They've kept some hotheads away from the uprisings, hotheads who just want trouble, not progress."

A few heads turned toward Boucher.

"Don't worry, Officer Boucher. We're not hotheads," Marnie said. "You can trust us. We can trust you."

"Yeah, we won't arrest you," someone joked.

"My granny wouldn't like it," Boucher replied. "You don't wanna mess with my granny."

Marnie continued. "Winter's coming. Our community has enough food and wood. This winter will be harder than last winter because the government will probably pull our funding for stopping that mine. We must help one another."

"We're with you, Marnie," someone said from the crowd. Many nodded or said, "Yes," in agreement.

"Thanks. That's important. If we stick together, we can go far."

How far, Mike Vidic wondered as he looked around. This must have been what a partisan meeting felt like during the war. He remembered his grandfather's stories, always told with an invigorating tone. He felt invigorated in this crowd.

"We have many educated band members, and many educated people from the outside who want to help us. Many of them have similar fights in their territories. We have supported them and now they support us."

"We also have our Chilcotin traditions, of standing together when the going gets tough."

"The tough get going!" someone said in the crowd.

"Right, we gotta get going around here," Marnie said. "We don't expect any help from the government, but this time we don't expect the army or police to land on us, either."

"We can't go back to living in the bush as if the settlers aren't here. They're here, but they're changing. They're adopting some of our ways. We can adopt some of their ways. Together, we can have a better world for us all."

A cheer went up from the crowd.

"Now, each of our band councillors has a specialty: health, education, natural resources, welfare; but you all must help more than you are used to helping. The government has made us all dependant on it, for money, for direction, for lots of stuff we used to do, without government help. Now we'll depend on ourselves, on one another, on helpful people from outside. We'll help them as much as we can, too."

"I see a new world opening for us, but that world has many things our old world had," Marnie waxed. "We are the people we have been waiting for, to change the world!"

Another cheer.

Marnie nodded toward Albert Daniels, who rose to speak.

"Yo, Albert!" someone shouted.

"Yo yourself," Albert said. "You and your 'yo' are going to work, but this time not on some temporary brush clearing job or other government or forestry scam. I'm the band councillor in charge of administration, and we're going to organize ourselves to build on yesterday's victory."

"Right on, Albert."

"You said it," Albert continued. "We have enough food and wood for the winter, even if none of us earns a dollar this winter. That might happen, but our ancestors got along without money and we could if we had to."

"We're Indians. We barter," a woman's voice rose from the crowd, quoting the line from the film <u>Smoke Signals</u>.

Laughter rose from many parts of the crowd.

"We do barter," Albert said. "We do it all the time but we don't notice it. Last year I traded my snow machine to Randy David for a winter supply of meat and fish. I had no time to hunt and his machine was a wreck."

"Hey, Albert. I fixed that machine, using a couple parts from yours." It was Randy's voice.

A few chuckles in the crowd. Handy Randy. No wonder the women chased him.

At the back of the hall, Simon van der Waals wondered if he could make both machines dependable. He had some machining practice from university and mining, and a shop full of tools, including a lathe.

Albert was talking about building and machine maintenance, electricity, school teachers, how fast the roadblock victory news spread, and the importance of everyone offering their skills. People were listening intently. A serious tone descended as people realized that their roadblock victory had ended one thing, but that victory had begun another, bigger thing.

"I'd like to introduce Bruce Culloden," Albert concluded. "Some of you know him from court cases he has done, here and elsewhere. He's the lawyer who overturned the injunction last year. He took away the government's power to fine us over the roadblock."

Albert always explained things in words that the average person understood. Would Bruce?

"Hello, everyone. Before you all break into groups for Albert, and make plans with your band councillors, I want to say a couple things about the law."

A few people were drifting outside, but most were still listening, as if sensing a return of lost power.

"There is Chilcotin law and there is settler law," Bruce said. "No government ever had the authority to stop Chilcotin law and start settler law. It's the same anywhere in Canada, the United States, and in North and South America."

"They imposed this law on you, and on many indigenous people. Now you can throw off this law and return to your traditional law, but..."

Albert winced in his chair. Lawyer "buts" irritated him when he was with the government child welfare ministry, and lawyer "buts" still irritated him.

"But there have been so many changes since the settlers came that your traditional legal system needs more laws. These new laws don't fight your old laws. Neither do they fight your traditions. Your values are good, better than the settler values; but some settler laws might come in handy."

"Think of it as a truck. There were no trucks here in the old days, before the settlers came. They brought trucks, but these trucks only went to people who could afford them."

"You got that right!" came from someone in the crowd.

"A truck is useful in many ways: haul a moose out of the bush, get to town...."

"To the casino!" someone said. A few laughed, nervously.

"Thanks for mentioning the casino," Bruce said. "Why do people go to the casino? They hope to win big money to buy stuff."

"Like a truck," someone said.

"Like a truck," Bruce echoed. "But what if we did what Albert says and bartered, shared the trucks? Then whoever needed one could use one without having to pay for it all by himself."

"It's called 'use value,'" Bruce said. "A truck is useful."

"There's also 'exchange value,' he continued. "A person can trade a truck for something else, like he traded money for the truck. Why do you pay twenty thousand for a truck? That's what the salesperson charges. You can bargain a bit, but not much."

"No kidding," came from the crowd.

"No kidding," Bruce echoed again. People seemed very interested in his story. Mike Vidic in the back of the gym had an idea where the story was going. Again, his grandfather with the Yugoslav partisans.

"Even that salesman has little say in how much to charge for the truck. He sells it, gets a percentage, and sends the rest of the money to the truck company's headquarters. The bosses pay the people who built the truck, but they keep some of the money for themselves. They even send some to shareholders. Those are people who each own part of the company that built the truck. But neither the bosses nor the shareholders actually helped build the truck. Still, they get more money than the people who did build the truck."

"That's not fair!" from the crowd.

Natural socialists, Culloden thought.

"To make a long story short, Chilcotin traditional law would treat the truck like Albert and Randy treated the snow machines. People who needed a truck would get together and buy one. Each person would use it when he or she needed it. Randy couldn't afford a new snow machine, so he borrowed Albert's. Randy paid by filling Albert's freezer with moose and fish."

"You can't use moose and fish to buy a truck from the dealer, but remember the people who built the truck and got paid less than their bosses and the company shareholders. Now, if the truck builders owned the company, they would get all the money from the truck sales. I don't say that we can pay them in moose and fish, but if there are no bosses or shareholders keeping some of the money, then we could probably buy a truck for less money."

"Remember that people sell moose and fish. If trucks were cheaper, then a person wouldn't have to sell so much moose and fish to buy a truck. Also, he might have a say in how much to charge for the truck. All the indigenous people in Canada together have lots of moose and fish. They also have lots of money.

"I don't!" a woman's voice said from the crowd. "The bosses and shareholders took mine!"

Culloden chuckled. "You catch on quick. Perhaps you could go to the truck factory to negotiate for us."

"Cool," a different woman's voice said from the crowd.

Chapter Three: Money Listens

The long meeting over, Holly and her Uncle Albert brought Sarah to Albert's house by the lake. Their ulterior motive was Sarah's bannock and drymeat, but Sarah came to watch the evening news on television. Her cabin had no television.

"I heard you say, 'Cool' at the meeting, Holly," Sarah said. "What's cool?"

"It's complicated," Holly replied.

Sarah frowned. "Young lady, life is complicated. Arguing on a roadblock is complicated. Your life is complicated. Try me. I'll stretch my brain to understand."

Holly blushed. "Sorry, Sarah. It's just that you've been through so much lately that I don't want to add more. But if you insist."

"When that lawyer was talking about the cost of trucks and who gets the money for building them, and who should get the money for building them, something clicked in my head. You know that I can drive anything on wheels. You probably also know that payments on my new logging truck almost bankrupt me every month."

"Now that I know we can do something about truck prices, without hurting the people who make trucks, I think things will get better for me."

"I understand," Sarah said. "I remember what the lawyer said about trucks, but he wasn't just talking about trucks there."

"Huh?" Holly said.

"Now it's your turn to understand something, Holly," Sarah said. "For generations, our people have been paying too much and getting too little back, and not just for trucks."

"I think what the lawyer meant was that we can get together to make a lot of things better for us all. When Rosalee spouted off and the lawyer suggested sending her to negotiate at the truck factory, I realized that a truck factory isn't the only place we can go to improve things for us. I also realized that if all the Indians in Canada got together, then we could improve things for everyone."

Holly thought about Randy. She still didn't know why it didn't work out between them. She wondered what Sarah thought about that.

"That lawyer is a white man, Holly; but he is with us. I think that many other white are with us, too."

Albert came from the kitchen, bannock and dry meat on a plate in one hand, teapot and cups in his other hand.

"You're a good waiter, Albert," Sarah said. "Make someone a good wife."

Albert thought of late Paula, his wife, who died of bile duct cancer at 32. They met when he was fresh out of university and took a job working for her people, the Athabasca Cree First Nation. What pollution they endured in Fort Chipewyan, from the tarsands upriver at Fort Macmurray. She was such an eloquent speaker, and fearless. When she talked, oil opportunists listened. Her people contracted an Irish doctor to study the health effects of the tarsands, but the provincial government vilified him into exile. Still, Paula's people wrested some control over their medical system. They decided which professionals, some from their own people, served them. Health outcomes were improving, but too late for Paula. She was cancerous before they moved together to Nemiah, where people instantly liked her straight talk and colorful humor. Chilcotins rarely liked Crees. They missed her almost like one of their own.

"There are plenty of Crees around here," the joke went. "They're all near the friendship centres, where they're safe."

Albert would like a say in how the Cariboo medical system worked. It hadn't worked for his dear Paula. Doctors delayed and misdiagnosed until it was too late for even the Vancouver Cancer Centre to save her. He had buried his bitterness in activism. As he listened from his kitchen, though, he realized that if he could send Randy to a far away truck factory, then he could send someone to the doctors' association to suggest better ways to interact with Indians. Albert felt less bitter today than he had felt in years. He was sorry he blasted Bruce. Good lawyer, that guy. I suppose there are good lawyers.

"You got anyone in mind for me to marry, Sarah?" Albert asked. "Remember, I'd be the husband."

"Yeah, she'd let you do a few things, Albert," Sarah grinned. "I'll see who I can find. The moccasin telegraph is full of surprises."

Albert put the plate, teapot, and cups on the coffee table and turned on the television.

The national news was starting, and they were on it.

Sarah was in the middle of the picture, chained to the propane tanks. She was talking to Officer Boucher. The commentator was talking about the history of the battle over the mine, Chilcotin resistance, unemployment, attempts to mediate before the roadblock went up, and the turning around of the mining trucks.

Settler news bias, paid for by Canadian taxpayers.

The camera showed the trucks leaving, then cut to Prime Minister Knight.

"Hey, it's that woman who came here last year," Sarah said. "She was pretty nervous when she was here."

"She was trying to get us to vote for her to be premier," Albert said. "I don't think anyone did. Gotta give her credit for trying, though. Putting those other guys in government didn't help us much, either."

"If she lost, then why is she still in charge?" Holly asked.

"She's Prime Minister, in charge of all of Canada now," Albert said.

"Hmmm," Sarah said.

Amy Knight had lost the provincial election, but the prime minister had lost his job over his crooked dealings with oil and mining companies. It started with a simple expense scandal in the senate, but that was a media circus to distract from bigger misuse of public money elsewhere in government. The prime minister wasn't the only guy responsible, or even the main guy; but he took the fall so his government would survive. Amy Knight was the shiny new face on that government.

From his origins leading an anti-tax group, to his takeover of a federal political party, Evan Brown had been like Shakespeare's tragic King Macbeth. He reached too far for too much power, and embarrassed himself and the country. Unlike Macbeth, however, Brown did not go broke or die. Still, there was a cauldron of public heat over how Knight rewarded Brown for helping her help his government. Shiny-faced Amelia Knight the scourge of government corruption had made Evan Brown Special Advisor to the Prime Minister on Natural Resources, Economics, and Taxation.

A growing movement for proportional representation ballooned upon news of that seedy sinecure. The 26% of Canadian voters who had voted for Brown's party and given him a majority government mostly defected to join the 74% who either voted against him or didn't vote at all. Barring an increasingly-likely socialist revolution, the next election would be proportional, not first-past-the-post.

Former Prime Minister Brown's ideas contradicted those of most Canadians, but people knew where he stood. His lightweight successor was different.

This new prime minister, a telegenic former newscaster and provincial premier, was as slippery as she was sexy. The slippery lost her premiership. The sexy made her federal party leader and therefore prime minister, but this battle seemed too much for her and her special advisor.

The announcer's voice cut in as Prime Minister Amy Knight talked about law and order. "Prime Minister Amelia Knight knows about the Chilcotin people. She was even in Nemiah when she was Premier of British Columbia."

"My government insists on the rule of law. This roadblock is merely the result of a failure in communication. The situation in Quebec is more serious, but again, we insist on a legal approach. Confrontation helps nobody."

"It sure helped today," Holly said.

"Yeah," Albert said. "But even law can help us. The Supreme Court ruled in our favor on the land claim. Now the government must sit down with us, respectfully."

"She still looks nervous," Sarah said, as the scene changed to downtown Montreal. A sea of people was marching toward the Olympic Stadium.

"In related news," the voice said, "an overflow crowd marched to the Olympic Stadium for a mass meeting called by a coalition of groups. The groups represent indigenous people, environmentalists, unions, women, and public servants, including Hydro Quebec workers."

"The march was peaceful but the meeting was not. Montreal police arrested more than 30 people who tried to disrupt the mass meeting. Some were anarchists, but most were from the fringe political party Tim Buck's Legacy. Its main branches are in Montreal, Toronto, Edmonton, and Vancouver."

What had been one tiny clutch of Canadian communists for most of the time since its 1921 founding had split into two catty factions in the early-1960s. A recent reunion of the competing cults, born of opportunism kindled by the economic crisis, their gospels jimmied together opportunistically, had produced this tiny new group. Like every religion, Tim Buck's Legacy had all the answers. Why listen to others, like the Quebec multitudes that wanted to be a vanguard, not be a vanguard's docile bludgeon against the corporate state and its government pets?

The camera panned to a group of people of various ages happily chanting "Timbucktu, la place pour vous" as police bundled the provocateurs into vans.

"Several municipal and provincial police, and soldiers from Valcartier Canadian Forces Base were on the podium, with the activist leaders."

The camera zoomed into the stage, where three officers stood. An English voiceover translated the French words.

"We soldiers of the Valcartier base protest the government's rough handling of protesters. We voted to stay in our barracks until negotiations replace attacks on unarmed people."

"The Montreal city police and Quebec provincial police support our stand. We three forces will resist any attempts to attack demonstrators in Quebec."

The commentator said, in a grave voice, "This is Canada's most serious crisis ever. Prime Minister Knight has a delicate line to walk. Her government hangs in the balance. Without the loyalty of the army and police, who will keep order?"

"Without the army here in 1864, we'd still control our land," Albert said. "This is an interesting time to be alive, for sure."

"I'm glad I lived to see it," Sarah said.

Now another voice narrated the tale of Dream Metals' bankruptcy. The camera showed stock footage of Simon van der Waals and Mike Vidic leaving a directors' meeting, looking harried. That was last week's news, very old now.

"I guess the tv people don't want to let those mining guys have a say," Holly said. "I think they're on our side now."

The voice noted the "dangerous financial exposure" of two chartered banks, which held much stock in Dream Metals, other mining companies, oil companies, and rail and trucking companies.

"Exposure, all right," Albert said. "Let 'em freeze, those banks."

"I wonder if we could send someone to talk for us at the banks?" Holly asked. "That Mike Vidic looks pretty sharp. And he needs a job now, with his mining company kaput."

"Hmm...." Albert said.

"We'll be right back," the woman newscaster said, "with a story about 'Balloons for Breast Cancer,' a Hamilton charity run by ex-steelworkers.

"Harrumph!" Albert said. He brought the empty dishes back to the kitchen, grumbling about privatized medicine and about charity, rather than taxation, funding medical research.

"I've seen enough," Sarah said. "Holly, would you push me home, please? It was nice to visit, Albert. Thanks for the tea."

"Thanks for the bannock and dry meat," came Albert's voice from the kitchen. "Yours is the best, Sarah."

"I'll gladly push you home," Holly told Sarah. Holly was nervous because Randy would probably be there, but she'd just drop Sarah off. She wanted to go see those mining men.

The harvest moon glowed reddish above the horizon, as the two women made their way in the chilly air.

"There's no light like moonlight, Holly," Sarah said. "The old people say that it makes people get along better."

"The old people," Holly pondered. Here's Sarah, the oldest person here, talking about the old people. But Holly knew that Sarah meant the old people who had passed on, the people whom the living remembered. It was as if nobody died here, or at least no memory died. Holly saw something important in that, but she couldn't put it into words. Randy sometimes had good words, like Granny Sarah had.

"Here we are, Sarah," Holly said. They heard footsteps inside. Randy opened the door.

"Hello, Randy."

"Hello, Holly."

"Good meeting, eh?"

"Yeah."

Sarah looked from one to the other and finally said, "Well, gotta get to bed for my beauty sleep."

"I gotta get wood," Randy brushed past them. Sarah looked at Holly.

"Goodnight, Sarah," Holly said, and turned to go.

"Moonlight, Holly," Sarah said. "Remember the magic of moonlight."

Magic schmagic, Holly thought, as she went to the band's log house bed and breakfast where Simon and Mike were staying. The lights were on. Good.

Holly knocked on the door. Simon answered.

"Hello..." he searched his memory for Holly's name.

"Holly," Holly helped.

"You drive trucks, don't you?" Simon asked.

"Yep. May I come in to talk about something?"

"Sure," Simon moved aside. Inside, Mike was typing on a laptop, the tv tuned to the same channel as in Albert's house.

One-channel Nemiah. You'd never know we had satellite tv out here, Holly thought. Everyone seemed to watch the few stations that have been here since antennas, since peasant vision, since rabbit ears.

Mike looked up from his laptop. "Hello."

"Hello," Holly said, sensing Mike's piercing blue eyes.

"Have a seat," Simon interrupted. Holly sat in a chair across the room from the men. "What did you want to talk about?"

"Well, it's complicated," Holly said, remembering the exchange with Sarah. She added quickly, "but I think you'll understand."

"We're all ears," Mike said, closing his laptop.

Holly took a deep breath.

"At the meeting today, the lawyer talked about trucks. You might know that I drive big trucks. He said that there's a way for us to have a say in how much they cost, and how much to pay the people who build them."

"I remember," Simon said.

"Well," Holly continued, "Albert, Sarah, and I were watching the news at Albert's place before I came here. Sarah said something that got me thinking."

Simon smiled. "That's no surprise. Sarah's pretty sharp. She said things that got me thinking, too."

Holly pressed on. "One news story was about the banks in trouble because they had stock in your company and other mining companies. I'm sorry about your company going bankrupt."

"Thanks, Holly," Mike said, anticipating the direction of Holly's story.

"Well, Albert thinks we could send someone to a truck factory, to talk for us" Holly said. "I asked him if we could send someone to a bank, to talk for us."

Mike Vidic sensed a new career landing in his lap.

Simon said, "Holly, I'll let Mike answer that. I'm more of an engineer. He's the financial whiz."

Holly looked at Mike. Mike took a deep breath and began.

"Do you know anyone who went bankrupt?"

"Man, do I ever," she replied. "My friend Rosalee Iqallie had truck payments and mortgage payments and lost her driving job when her mill closed. The bank took everything: logging truck, house, the works. Even her husband Walter left her. Now he's on the streets in Williams Lake and she's working at Dairy Queen. She can't borrow a cent for three more years. She's the one who heckled the lawyer at today's meeting. She's the one he offered to send to the truck factory."

Mike sensed an opening.

"That's bankruptcy, all right," he said. "Even companies go bankrupt. You probably had a few go bankrupt in the Cariboo."

What an understatement, Holly thought. The Cariboo, last one out turn off the light and close the door. She was glad she still had a job. She hoped she still had a job. What would she do if her mill, the last in Williams Lake, closed?

"Well, even banks can go bankrupt," Mike said.

"About time," Holly said. "Get their own medicine back. But who takes them over? They're banks. They usually take over bankrupt people and businesses."

"People can take over banks," Mike answered. "You know about credit unions."

No shit, Shirley, Holly thought. Try to get a loan from that bunch of hags.

"Credit unions are run by the people whose money they have. Banks are bigger than credit unions, and they're run by people who have shares in them."

Holly remembered Lawyer Bruce talking about shareholders. "Bruce talked about shareholders in the truck factory." To heck with banks. Holly wanted to run a truck factory. Trucks were something she understood. Perhaps the band council would send her and Rosalee to a truck factory.

"Same idea," Mike said. "People who have money in banks can take them over. In fact, the biggest bank in Quebec is a credit union. It's called Caisse des Peuples, "Bank of the People," and it has been in the news all week. It's in trouble, too, but its members might have a solution, one that could work for banks."

"To make a long story short, if the two chartered banks that have mining stocks go bankrupt, then the people with money in the banks could take them over. I understand that your band and many bands have money in one of those banks."

Holly remembered the cheques she got for hauling logs for the band's new houses last year. "Royal Bank," she thought aloud.

"Well, if that bank goes bankrupt, then you all might make a deal with it to take it over. You could get it for cents on the dollar."

Holly remembered the pittance that Scotiabank had given Rosalee when she went bankrupt. Then the bank sold her truck and house for much more than it had given Rosalee. Crooks.

"You could send someone to the Williams Lake of branch of Scotiabank. Indians elsewhere could send someone to other branches. Your national assembly could send someone to the Toronto headquarters. Not only Indians have money in Scotiabank and Royal Bank, but you could have a say in how to run the banks that have your money. Foreigners have money in these banks, too."

   A third bank, the Bank of Montreal, owns a big chunk of a railway that used to be publicly owned. Foreigners own part of that railway, too. Neither the bank nor the railway is in good financial shape lately. Their misfortune is your opportunity."

   None of Canada's five chartered banks was thriving, unlike Canada's credit unions. The banks had lent money easily, able to cover domestic losses using lucrative foreign income from mines, among other things. Lacking this financial cushion, credit unions had been more careful, more by necessity than by good ethics. The foreign income cushions of the chartered banks were fast becoming financial millstones dragging their balance sheets into seas of red ink.

   Holly understood, as she had understood at today's meeting.

   Simon looked at Mike. Mike looked at Simon.

   "What?" Holly asked. "I get it." Then, seeming to read Mike's mind, she said, "You sound pretty smart about banks, Mike. We could send you to Williams Lake, or even to the bank's regional office in Prince George, or even to higher offices."

   "Of course, the band council would have to approve it. I could ask Albert to bring it up at the next meeting, which is tomorrow afternoon."

   Holly got up. "Thanks for everything. Gotta go. You guys here for awhile?"

   "We hope so," Simon said. "It's not as if I have a mining company to go run anymore."

   "Sorry about that," Holly said. "We didn't mean to drive you out of business."

   "Thanks," Simon said, "but Dream Metals was on the ropes already. Its mines in Africa and Latin America brought it more trouble than you did here. It might be for the best."

   It sure might be for my best, Mike Vidic thought, as Holly closed the door behind her.

   "Good work, Mike," Simon said. "You might have just found a new career."

   "That's exactly what I was thinking," Mike said.

   "Great minds think alike. Fools seldom differ," Simon said. "Now, off to bed I go. See you in the morning."

"Goodnight."

Holly walked home in the moonlight, aglow.

Chapter 4: The Centre Cannot Hold

Holly, Rosalee, Albert, and Bruce opined about sending someone to a truck factory to have a say in truck pricing and what to pay the people who make trucks. The people who make trucks have been making something other than trucks since two of the big three automakers declared bankruptcy. They plan to return to making trucks, for themselves and the people who need them, not for the shareholders sideswiped by United States and European bank and government financial crises.

Daimler Chrysler fell first, and its parent company Daimler Benz in Germany could not do a darn thing to save it. First, Deutches Bank collapsed, soaked in Greek debt that the Greeks finally refused to repay. This was "odious debt," called that because the government that contracted it cut educational and social programs to try to repay it. The borrowed money hadn't served the people.

Bolivian economist Arturo Garcia had popularized the phrase in Latin America, but the United States itself had defaulted on what it called "odious debt" to Spain contracted by Cuba, Philippines, and Puerto Rico after it wrested them from Spanish control by war in the late-1890s. Uncle Sam was not one to preach. Latin America had certainly stopped listening, the Bolivarian Revolution having spread through the continent, even to pro-U.S. Colombia and its comprador elite.

Mexican auto workers took this as a cue to occupy Ford plants on their side of the Texas border. There were even public and government rumblings about returning Texas, Arizona, New Mexico, and adjacent states that the U.S. had captured by arms in the 1840s. Ford endured, but barely, its books still hidden from government auditors in the U.S. and elsewhere: all those ties to the Hitler Nazi government during World War Two were skeletons in a Ford closet, whose financial hinges seemed to be falling off.

The U.S. military now found itself overextended in foreign wars of aggression and unable to muster enough soldiers, enough loyal soldiers, to keep order at home.

The U.S. government had refused German pleas for help against the revolutions in Greece, Italy, and Portugal that scuttled debt repayment from them, and scuttled Germany's flagship bank. Now Daimler Chrysler twisted in the financial wind.

General Motors fell to bankruptcy next, this bankruptcy home-grown. It had opened its books to government auditors, in hopes of a second bailout. The 2009 bailout had taught neither it nor its bank creditors lessons in financial prudence. Derivative trading in its finance arm, leveraged buyouts of various suppliers, building military vehicles on the shaky credit for government contractors and the government itself, hiring shadowy paramilitary outfits to police its unruly factories at home and abroad. What was good for General Motors had turned out not to be good for it, nor for America.

No bailout came, from a government itself in hock to China for industrial output and currency debt, and Russia for mineral and fossil fuel imports. Both countries had fresh new communist governments, but the autocracy of Lenin, Stalin, and Mao guided few in or out of power in those countries. Ignorant nostalgic fanatics such as Stalin's Legacy continued to harp their one-note symphony of sanctimony in Canada, as a few similar, small, laughable groups did in the US and Europe. These new improved Reds owed more to Trotsky and especially to Rosa Luxemburg than to the pseudo-religious autocratic cabals that had foisted unwanted, damaging, and oppressive answers on generations in the twentieth century.

The debt-laden US government had had little choice but to let the banks fail. Banks that had been called "too big to fail" a decade earlier showed themselves quite able to fail. Wall Street financial houses had proven their foundations too brittle to enable them pick the banks' carcasses.

As in 1780s France, a sclerotic financial sector had broken rather than bent. As in 1780s France, the powerful had ignored voices of moderation who howled loudly as the crisis spread. Unlike in 1790s France, no bloody dictatorship emerged to cut the head off this revolution.

United States President Winona McKay was a practical Kentucky woman who wouldn't let her country slide to tyranny, as her beloved Kentucky had been jackbooted into the Confederate side during the United States Civil War of 1861-1865.

A medical professor who had run the Bone Diagnostics and Research Laboratory at the Lexington campus, McKay knew what war could do and she wanted none of it. McKay's research had focused on war's effects on the body, current wars and past wars. Her pro-Union ancestors had suffered for their stand against the Southern Slave States. Working with university archaeologists, McKay had analyzed exhumed bodies from that tragic but necessary war. She always wondered if any of those bones were from her ancestors.

Politics had come to her. She had not gone to it. When congress and the senate impeached Republican President Tom Sherman for bogging the country down in an unauthorized war against Iran, Democratic Leader Alex Foster had refused to take the job. Sherman, a conservative speaker and writer from Detroit, had spoken and written his way to the state governorship. Sherman's evisceration of Michigan's public sector had driven thousands of teachers, students, government workers, immigrants, and industrial workers to the streets.

Sherman's reactionary eloquence had gained him the national party leadership. The growing financial crises, and the media circus that is US politics had gained him the US presidency. Media eagerly ate their own when Sherman tried against Iran what he had done against Michigan. Not one soldier's boot hit Iranian soil: congress and senate members facing strong anti-war movements at home had impeached Sherman.

Democratic Leader Alex Foster pined for the silver screen that had made him famous before politics conscripted him. Unlike Ronald Reagan, this Hollywood icon was pro-union: no Screen Actors purges for this hometown boy from Everett, Washington. Foster's ancestors had some ancestors in the International Workers of the World, the "Wobblies."

Alex Foster's great-grandfather had been on the boatload of Wobblies fired on by Everett vigilantes and police on November 5, 1916. Had the bullet been a bit closer Grandpa Lars Svenson's carotid artery, Alex Foster would not be around today. Alex knew the story well, from Grandma Foster. Alex also knew the poverty that Lars endured when the headaches from the wound made finding and keeping a job difficult.

Medicare, finally proper medicare, had been a major plank in Foster's run for the Democratic Party leadership. The health maintenance organizations and insurance companies had pulled every string of every political and economic puppet they had, but Foster had won the leadership. His action-hero physique and bright blond hair had helped. The anti-medicare rhetoric continued. It helped elect Sherman, narrowly.

When Sherman's words and deeds undid him, Alex Foster said that he would only assume the presidency in a coalition government, a coalition of more parties than only Democrats and Republicans. Fearing that Foster would bring "a nest of socialists" into government, as Franklin Delano Roosevelt had done in the 1930s, the Democrats refused his offer. Enter Winona McKay, Foster's vice presidential running mate in the losing 2016 election. She agreed to run the party if Foster stayed on as her vice presidential running mate for 2020.

Foster had agreed, reluctantly at the time; but the growing crisis was growing ideas in his head. His sprouting ideas might make Great-Grandpa Lars Svenson proud. Even if this government wanted to "save capitalism" as Roosevelt's had done decades earlier, could it? No loss to Foster if it couldn't. His cousins in Sweden happily paid high taxes and got something for them. Low US taxes brought war and poverty at worst, "the cold hand of charity" at best.

Grandma Foster never liked Roosevelt, Alex remembered. "My dad wanted a new world in the New World," she often said. "He didn't leave a monarchy of inheritance to die in a monarchy of money," she said, sometimes in Swedish, sometimes in English. "That's not what brought him and Joe Hillstrom to America."

Great-Grandpa Lars had been one of the people who had carried Hillstrom, "Joe Hill," across the Utah state line in 1916. Joe didn't want to rest in peace in the state whose government had shot him by firing squad to please its copper mining bosses.

Winona McKay knew and trusted Alex Foster. She trusted him more than the party's old guard that had refused his coalition offer. Was now the time for a coalition government? It was an easier sell now, as the old guard's power faded like the dividends on their stocks.

A public servant herself, McKay had helped increase university access for low income and immigrant students at the University of Kentucky. Her eidetic memory replayed the university's mission statement:

> The University of Kentucky is a public, land grant university dedicated to improving people's lives through excellence in education, research and creative work, service, and health care. As Kentucky's flagship institution, the University plays a critical leadership role by promoting diversity, inclusion, economic development, and human well-being.

"University for the smart, not for the rich," was the student strike slogan that the university's governors finally heeded. The University of Kentucky lived up to its mandate as a state university, open to all in the state, and beyond. Medical professorship had been a hard place to leave for national politics. How about "evidence-based" politics to replace the lobbyist-driven legerdemain that had dominated for decades, and now recently threatened to destroy the republic?

Tom Sherman indeed, marching destructively over peace and public services, as his namesake, Union Army General Sherman, had scorch-marched from Atlanta to the sea in 1865. Fixing his mess was a big reason she entered politics.

She wouldn't make the mistakes that Woodrow Wilson made when he descended from academia to politics more than a century ago. If she promised no war, there would be no war, unlike the cataclysm of World War One that Wilson foisted on the country. If she promised to rein in the banks, she would rein in the banks, unlike the Federal Reserve System that Wilson invented.

Bankers regulating themselves and the economy. Foxes regulating the chicken coop. The banks seemed easy to rein in now, being closer to dead horses than to vigorous horses, closer to bull shitters than to that Wall Street bull statue.

Occupy Wall Street's "Chisel Brigade" had dismantled that Bull on live television only fewer than three weeks ago, as Germans had dismantled the Berlin Wall fewer than three decades ago. Now people wore pieces of the bull as amulets, as people had put pieces of the Berlin Wall above their fireplaces. The amulets of the activists were growing strong enough to dissolve the Berlin Wall bricks and the mansions that housed them.

But an economy needs a financial system, McKay knew. Perhaps Foster's "nest of socialists" had some ideas.

Tonight's live national broadcast of her speech might galvanize some help. She sure needed it. The speech was good, if somewhat more radical than she anticipated. She remembered watching a podcast of F.D.R.'s speech during World War Two, a speech that advocated medicare, full employment, strong unions, financial regulation, and public services, and many measures that European governments built on the ashes of their bombed-out countries. Many of Roosevelt's proposals, and some that might make FDR wince, were in her speech. McKay had heard plenty about FDR from her elders, as a child in rural Kentucky.

Arguments about FDR's public works programs, and about the Civil War, had made Winona McKay think critically as a child and teen. She strived in school, and got that state scholarship that made university affordable. Others had been as smart as she was, smarter even; but the essay she sent to the scholarship committee, and her good Scholastic Aptitude Test score, had gotten her the scholarship.

One scholarship, one measly scholarship. So many others would have been as able as she was to excel at university. She got to "UK" eager to learn about healing the human body, her Kentucky such a historical laboratory of disease and death. She also arrived knowing rare she was, a poor kid among rich kids in academia. She didn't resent them, even the ones who felt that their family wealth entitled to be in university. Born on third base and think they hit a triple. She was there to learn, as most of them were.

As she rose through graduate school, McKay became eager to broaden access to university, first by increasing the number of scholarships and widening the range of people on scholarship committees, and second by reducing the tuition costs. The nationwide student strikes hadn't spared UK. A full tenured professor by then, McKay felt secure enough to advocate for the students. A grumbly university senate improved the scholarship system and lowered tuition. Probably some former coal company lawyers among that bunch. She remembered what lawyers had done to her mountainside village soon after she reached UK.

Winona McKay had climbed from a hillside coal town, whose people had been abruptly relocated, whose hill had been blasted away by "mountain top removal" coal companies, to the height of academia. Good riddance to those bankrupt blasters of mountains, and their lawyers. Helping the university brass see sense was edifying for McKay. If the coal companies had listened to Winona's mother and many others, the companies might have survived, instead of going down in a blaze of battles against health scientists, environmentalists, and their lawyers.

Winona's Grandpa McKay, with his coal dust cough, died two years after leaving the house where he had been born. He was so sad to move. She just knew that Grandpa would have lived longer in his quaint little house than in that Lexington social housing complex. She remembered visiting him there in her early university days. He was always so interested in her studies. Sharp old coot. His decline decided was yet another reason she wanted to study medicine. People can't live forever, but they can live better, in less pain, even as they age.

Grandpa's ancestors had been driven from their Scottish land by wool merchants and sheep lords. The proud crofters became wage slaving coal miners in the industrial revolution, or emigrants to America. Grandpa's McKay ancestors immigrated to the United States to mine coal. The New World paid better and had no lords, the Scots thought. Coal barons like the Peabody family erected a neo-European class structure in the smoky mountains.

Grandpa knew who he was, as did his granddaughter: each grew from the hard Kentucky soil and history. History connected them to their pasts and to each other.

"You connect things," Grandpa said. He'd ramble on about coal strikes in the old days, about company stores gouging people, about anti-union thugs, about the Tennessee Valley Authority, about everything from his world, from her roots. He'd connect them in story, if one had the patience to listen.

She had been young and full of herself, but Winona must have listened to Grandpa. She connected that past to her adolescence of hard study, that study to her scholarship, that scholarship to the many from her village who would have done just fine in university, to the lawyers who cleared off their families and hers, to the lawyers who brought down the coal companies, to the lawyers on the university board who listened to her. She had almost chosen law over medicine.

Connections, like bones connected in a body. She remembered the song from her childhood: "The neck bone's connected to the backbone; the backbone's connected to the leg bone...."

Grandpa coughed when he tried to sing the old union and gospel songs. Winona sang like a bird, in the valley church back home. She sang helping Mom pack up yet another bag of cast-off clothes for a family poorer than theirs. She sang helping Mom make a cake for a rag-dressed neighbor girl.

"Don't worry, little bird, I'll make you a cake when it's your birthday," Mom would say as the cake went from oven to counter to nearby shack.

"Little bird" sang in the school choir, and in the university choir. Her coiffed choir mates didn't know what to make of this girl with the funny expressions and coal-black hair who sang with them, this girl whom their boyfriends eyed from a row or two behind in the choir. Winona wasn't interested in men that way, yet. She had academic plans. Eventually she was friends with almost all the other women, in the choir, and their men.

"You gotta get along in this world, Little Bird," Mother always said. Her choir mates dropped their jealousy and sneering. They befriended Winona. More than once, one or the other of them cried on her shoulder about some man, some test, something or other. People came to her. People trusted her.

John Shays came to Winona McKay, in a project to unearth Civil War dead in Kentucky and adjacent states. Born in Concord, Massachusetts, Shays was descended from Daniel Shays, the leader of a 1780s rebellion against the national government fresh from throwing off English rule in the War of Independence. The new government was as oppressive as the English had been, more so in some ways, to Shays. He had helped dispatch British redcoats, their onerous taxmen, and debt collectors. He tried, and failed, to dispatch United States bluecoats and their financial masters.

Shays grew up in Concord, where Henry David Thoreau had retreated from the industrial world. Thoreau finally retreated from support for slavery, and even opposed the 1840s war that stole Mexican land to make Texas, New Mexico, and assorted other states.

Steeped in the past, Shays had gotten a scholarship to the University of Chicago. He emerged an archaeologist, a person with an ear for the stories of the past, stories told by bones, objects, and the mass of material left behind by generations whose lives are brief but whose legacy speaks to the trained ear. His doctorate fresh in hand, Shays hired on with the Field Museum.

Shays soon found himself among Nuu-chah-nulth people on Vancouver Island. They wanted their ancestors' bones back from the famous Chicago museum. It seemed that others had disputes with the dominant view of American history. Shays and Thoreau for him. Ancestors for these Indians from across the continent. He remembered the ceremonial loading onto a plane of the boxed bones, and their ceremonial reburial under the coastal rainforest canopy.

His next fieldwork for Field landed Shays in Winona McKay's exhumation of Civil War dead. He was the expert archaeologist whose fine ear heard the bones' stories more clearly than non-experts did. Bone breaks, punctures, burial positions and objects, a million clues, large and small, enhanced the research project that McKay oversaw. Work among the dead fertilized romance between the Kentucky professor and the Massachusetts scholar.

Rural people ponder what's over the horizon rather than endure the built urban environment's limits, and sometimes rural people make quite versatile scholars. This pair pondered each other.

McKay saw the lanky Yankee, and Shays saw the dark-haired Southerner. What a product of evolution he was, from the bony fingers to the big, clumsy feet. As Thomas Huxley, "Darwin's Bulldog" defending evolution, would agree, natural selection was an elegant wonder. What Shays lacked in physical grace he made up for in patience and humor.

When Shays first saw McKay, on her his eye "smoot, and ther it stente," as Geoffrey Chaucer wrote in the Medieval <u>The Story of Troilus</u>. The things a person remembers from a university English course when digging up dead soldiers alongside a dark-eyed southerner. Troilus the Trojan soldier and Criseyde the Greek princess was an unlikely match, as were Shays the Yankee anthropologist and McKay the Southern scientist.

    Scientific collaboration became as sensual as the dirt in which they dug. First they co-published. Then they co-habited. Smoot and stente all right. Chicago's loss was Lexington's gain when John Shays bundled his collection of bones, artifacts, and papers at Field into a rented truck and drove south to Lexington, and Winona. The University of Kentucky happily hired the bespectacled bone man whose enchanting teaching style soon filled its lecture halls, whose diligent research output soon enhanced the university's reputation.

    People come to me, McKay thought, remembering the choir girls' tales of heartbreak and John's tales of Vancouver Island Indians. People trust me, she thought.

    Would the millions of people who would see her speak on television tonight come to Winona McKay? Would they trust her?

    Peace not war, public service not privatization. Her party leadership campaign slogan might bring more cheers and fewer boos from millions in front of their televisions tonight than it had brought from the convention floor the night she became Alex Foster's Democratic running mate. Glad that phrase is in the speech.

    As she read the speech, President McKay thought, "A country needs a financial system. Ours doesn't seem to have one anymore. I hope there's someone watching tonight who's as good with banks and money as I am with bones and muscles."

    More and better regulations had kept Canada's banks afloat, but as mining companies sank at home and abroad, banks sank, like tailings sink to the bottom of a pond. What would Prime Minister Amelia Brown do? What could she do? What should she do? There was no lack of media blather about the problem, but little about possible solutions.

Maritime media mouth Lex Mitchell was on the Canadian Broadcasting Corporation television news almost every night, polysyllabically pontificating against this wrong policy or that wrong proposal. Give a guy a Rhodes scholarship and he thinks he's Joseph Schumpeter, economic exorcist, casting demons out of capitalism.

I cast thee out, in the name of Adam Smith, David Ricardo, and Milton Friedman, the father, son, and the holy ghost of capitalism. Meanwhile, the theses of Karl Marx, Thorsten Veblen, and Michael Parenti flapped in the wind on the cathedral door. Rotten door.

The crises had been good for autoworkers, in North America and elsewhere. With help from Argentines who were veterans of taking over abandoned factories, that now included a couple U.S.-owned auto plants, North American autoworkers were learning to run their own auto plants. "Management rights" was a quip for bygone days, not a whip for today. All workers had management rights now. Mid-level banking managers, refugees with rubber paycheques, were rolling up their financial sleeves and showing the autoworkers what had been long hidden up those sleeves.

Autoworkers were showing bankers solidarity, and Solidarity USA was the name of their vigorous new union. It had deposed, local by local and then at the national convention a month ago, the phalanx of porkers who had schmoozed with bosses, bankers, and government officials. People from the shop floor, people from the dealership floor, and now people from the bank floor had the happy courage to work together, on something worth working for, for all.

Underpaid and unpaid state police forces and National Guard units showed spectacularly little interest in quelling this new industrial revolution. State and federal cutbacks, and concession-heavy collective agreements had sowed winds of resentment, and now a whirlwind of change blew. Like a Lake Michigan storm blowing away dead dry leaves and cleaning the ground for the darling buds of May, Solidarity USA now blew new ideas, many of them really old ideas, across the country and beyond.

Chapter 5: Hills to Mills

"Wake up, Holly! We gotta go to town!"
It was Rosalee, fellow trucker, now on hard times slinging soft ice cream in the Williams Lake Dairy Queen. Staff were friendly and the work was fun, although it paid less than driving a logging truck. Still, it was indoor, year-round work. The only chaining up Rosalee did was chaining up her mouth when some whiny customer complained about this or that, or some snooty student working part time became a know-it-all, especially about Indians. "I don't wanna be part of anybody's experience," Rosalee had said more than once.

Honestly, the things a single mom endures for a paycheque. Her son Leon would graduate next spring, near the top of his class in Williams Lake's high school, a ridiculous concoction of two campuses which duplicated some courses and didn't offer others at all. Getting an education here was a good trick, especially for smart Indians. At least Leon had stopped shoving his fist and racist students' words down their throats. "Just say nothing," Rosalee advised. "They'll always be ignorant rednecks, but you can go to university and be anything you want."

Architecture? Architecture interested her precious 16-year-old son? Go figure. He had helped make sweat lodges by Konni Lake during summer jobs working with youth, but the photos he showed her: buildings made of straw bales, packed earth, recycled materials sprouting with a strange beauty from every face.

"Your ancestors lived in pit houses," she told her son. "I suppose they're packed earth. Going back to your roots, child?"

Leon the architect. Leon shared the name of an architect, Leon Wren, who designed St. Paul's Cathedral in London, England. Leon had read about Wren, who used 17th-century technology and techniques to build remarkable, lasting buildings. He wanted to make lasting things.

His middle name was , after the Chilcotin warrior who tried to enforce Chilcotin law when settlers illegally occupied Chilcotin land in the 1860s. The settlers, mostly from England and the United States, had ignored Chilcotin law, sexually enslaved Chilcotin women, and intentionally infected Chilcotin people with diseases to which they had little natural immunity. Most of the people had died. English law then declared "terra nulles," "empty land," to legalize its "preemption" of that land for settlers. Legal genocide? Such a legal system had no right to exist then, and has none now. Happily, that system was in decline, sinking with the sinking economic system it had defended for generations. Violence and trickery had defeated the Chilcotin legal system, but now the victors were becoming the vanquished. A hybrid legal system would emerge, combine the best of both systems, and people would build a better world. Leon the architect would build housing and much else in that world.

  Leon Iqallie, student of the past, builder of the future.

  There is a continuity of memory, whose destruction is an impossible challenge to even the harshest of despots. When a few people survive invasion, rape, attempted genocide, abuse by residential schools, other prisons, and the governments and moneyed interests who support them and buy and pay for those governments; when a few survive, memory survives, memory of better times possible, in the past and in the future.

  Even when a tyrant kills all foes, as happened to indigenous people in various parts of the world, including Canada, tyranny inspires a quest for freedom, for justice. The last Beothuk died, in Newfoundland, in the 1820s; but the mercantile enslavement of the next occupants of Newfoundland recently died as well. As in the rest of Canada and the world, people were breaking the economic and mental chains that had seemed so permanent so recently.

  People have ideas, but ideas also spring from conditions. A bright new crop of ideas was springing from conditions in Newfoundland, in Nemiah, and countless other places, near and far.

  Leon, a name that spoke of roots.

  Rosalee was about to root out Holly.

―――――――――

Holly sleepily opened the door. "What's up? What the heck time is it? This is a day off for me."

"Nope. You and I are going to work."

"Huh?"

"We're going to town. While you were watching the news in the bed and breakfast last night, which that handsome young mining guy, I was on the phone."

No secrets around here, Holly thought. Can't even watch the news with someone without a flock of busybodies marrying you off to him.

"I called the union. Actually, Carl called me."

Carl Schultz was the German-born Williams Lake secretary of a union that included two million workers in wood, hydro-electricity, oil, steel, auto parts, government services, education, and much else. He came from a socialist Germany and told anyone who would listen that he wanted a socialist Canada. More and more were listening.

"They're changing the union into management," Rosalee said. That is, they plan to take over the Williams Lake mill, and maybe bring the dead mills back to life. I could leave the ice cream racket for something really cool. Carl said that we'd have more say in how to run the place."

"I'm there," Holly said. "Let me wash up and get dressed."

Just like when they were little girls, Holly thought. Some aunt or mother or grandmother would be sitting around one minute. The next minute, she would order the girls to get ready to go, and be quick about it. Such women had two speeds: neutral and overdrive. She preferred the subtlety of her 20-speed logging truck.

A subtle logging truck?

Five minutes later, Holly emerged from the bathroom, pony tail swinging, backpack hanging from one shoulder, glint in her eye.

"What?" Holly replied to Rosalee's raised eyebrow.

"This doesn't surprise me," Holly said. "What we talked about last night in the bed and breakfast is sort of related."

"Tell me more," Rosalee grinned. "Cute guy, that miner."

"Get stuffed! It wasn't like that. Get your mind out of the ditch, trucker."

In the early morning light outside Holly's house, there stood the band's 14-passenger van, with three passengers in it.

"My noise box little car has today off," Rosalee explained. "No Dairy Queen for me anymore. There are enough teenagers to run that place. They might make a co-op out of it, given the American financial crash. I think Dairy Queen crashed, too."

Two back seats had been removed from the van to make room for Sarah David's wheelchair. Randy sat in the seat in front, Albert in the seat in front of that. Each had a mass of papers beside him.

"Morning, Holly," Sarah chirped. "Nice moonlight last night, eh?"

Holly wasn't awake enough for this topic, yet. Neither, it seems, was Randy, who grunted a hello and returned to talking to Albert.

Rosalee took the wheel, Holly the front passenger seat.

Albert leaned forward as they drove along the lake to leave Nemiah.

"Thanks for coming, Holly. Rosalee and you will pick up Felix Essex at Stone, drop us off in Anaham, and pick up Erin Marseille there, and Chief Peter Wajda in Toosey, on your way to town. Today will be a big day. I'm glad that Nemiah is organized enough for me to attend today's meetings."

"Meetings?" Holly asked.

"Today, there will be two meetings in Anaham, the first in the gym, the second in the Chilcotin Cultural Centre. People are coming from as far away as Bella Coola and Canoe Creek: indigenous, settlers, lots of people. We hope to form a Cariboo-Chilcotin regional government, to deal directly with the federal government."

"What about the British Columbia Treaty Commission?" Rosalee asked. "The Shuswaps stuck themselves in that ridiculous outfit. They talk to the provincial government."

"Why talk to the monkey when you can talk to the organ grinder?" Sarah said from her perch. The Shuswaps were about to leave the treaty commission, finally.

"There might not be a provincial government much longer," Albert continued. "I heard that Ottawa is convening a constitutional conference to make one powerful national government composed of people from regional governments," Albert explained, remembering the flood of emails he had read the day before.

"Today's Anaham meeting is part of organizing a Cariboo-Chilcotin regional government, to enhance and probably replace the Cariboo Regional District."

"Now, if you'll excuse me, I want to sleep a bit. I was up late last night. Wake me up at Stone, Randy." Albert fluffed a pillow and leaned his head against the outside of the van, as Rosalee drove it out of the hills and toward Henry's Crossing, the bridge across the Taseko River.

"I'm a little bagged, too, Rosalee," Holly said. "Mind if I sleep a bit?"

"Go right ahead," Rosalee said. "I want you sharp for Williams Lake today. We'll probably stay at my brother's place. I'm glad you brought a bag."

Holly knew to be prepared. It was how her people survived generations under settler rule, rule now fading fast.

The van rumbled along the 90 kilometres of gravel road that led to Highway 20 and Lee's Corner.

Anaham Chief Cara Marseille looked around the gym. The tables were set up. The kitchen bustled with food preparation. School children were hanging posters and other artwork on the walls, and sculptures on the tables. Her dad Marvin was directing the youth, her mom Erin shuttling between band office and gym. Cara's daughter Rebecca trailed around after the older children, carrying this and helping with that. Her toddler son Kevin shadowed Marvin as he helped other children erect their sculptures, some metal, some wood, some both, as centrepieces on the tables.

Long-time truck driver Marvin Marseille, like Marnie Triste at Nemiah, had a French last name. The Oblate priests who practically ran his land when he was a boy had a statue in Marseille, France. The statue was of Eugene de Mazenod, the Oblates' founding father, yet another Ultramontane from the mid-nineteenth century whose zeal spread Catholicism to distant lands. The statue was still there, but the church that housed it was now an African culture centre, in that Mediterranean coastal city that was 45% African.

Finally, the French had expropriated church property, as their 1789 revolution had failed to do. A few priests and churches still operated, but the Maratist Party government had so increased economic equality that few people pined for a heavenly hereafter, the here-now being so much better than before the change of government.

Finally, a few years before that, the Chilcotins had bid farewell to the order of nuns that had been in Anaham since the 1940s. Marvin was glad the band didn't tear down the convent. Now it was a cultural centre. If a French city that wasn't even half African could make a church into a cultural centre, then a Canadian community that was 90% Chilcotin could make a convent into a cultural centre.

He'd go check a few things there this morning, to be sure that cheery, renovated building was ready for today's second meeting. Indigenous people from all over the world came there. It promoted Chilcotin culture, and had increased the pride of Anaham elders, the diligence of Anaham children. Heck, his wife Erin's addictions job was more public relations than trenchant intervention now, with 90+% sobriety in the community.

"Dad, how do you think it will go today?" Cara asked at his elbow.

"Let the people talk, Cara. They'll do the right things, after they argue until they're out of breath."

My opinionated people, Cara thought. Only last month, the clan-based band council had appointed her chief for this year. There was lots she didn't know, but the council worked together better than the old councils had. It was clan-based, not clannish. Ottawa's devolution of many powers a few years ago had included electoral power.

Anaham had almost immediately replaced the rancorous system of voting for individual councillors with a system in which each of the six main families chose two people to sit in the band government. This was similar to what the Six Nations did in Ontario and Quebec, but unlike there, Anaham implemented the system without having to stare down the federal government. Any rancor was in the families choosing their two people, not in the operation of the council.

Things got done better than in her dad's day. Houses went up. The cultural centre, his pride and joy, was an international showpiece. The band ran the health system for everyone between the Fraser River and the Coastal Mountains. Albert Daniels was currently trying to get Chilcotin influence into the tired old medical system in Williams Lake, where the hospital was. She'd be glad to see Albert today. She had ideas for him. She knew he'd have ideas for her.

———

Dozens, children, adults, elders, cheered as the van stopped at the Stone band office.

Randy nudged Albert awake. "We're famous, Albert."

"I'm famous, Randy. I was on the news last night," Sarah said. "People probably want my autograph. See the sign?"

Two small girls held a banner that said, "Super Sarah, said 'No' to mine-iacs."

Holly, already awake, looked around for Felix Essex, Sarah's cousin and a respected elder in the community. Being respected in this community meant much. For the "Stone" Chilcotins stuck fast to their traditions. They had done so since anthropologist Livingston Ferrand wrote about their ancestors in <u>Chilcotin Indian Legends</u> in 1900. One of those traditions was to respect elders, elders worthy of respect. One of those elders was Felix Essex. Only his surname was English, from English remittance men who grabbed nearby land in the 1870s. The rest of Felix was pure Chilcotin.

Felix Essex bounded down the road from his little house, carrying his guitar case.

"Hello, Sarah. Hello, everyone. Mind if I bring my guitar?"

"Nope," Randy said. "Today will probably inspire a song or two."

Felix on board, the van wound down the road to the bridge across the Chilcotin River. A few minutes later, it rolled into Anaham, where another, larger crowd cheered, by the school.

Felix and Albert got out. Randy unhitched Sarah's wheelchair. Rosalee unfolded the lift, rolled Sarah onto it, and lowered her to the ground.

Chief Cara Marseille looked at Sarah as if she had just defeated the British Army. "Welcome, Sarah. I'm so glad you're here."

Holly talked to children gathered around the van. Teenage girls hung on her every word about the roadblock.

"You have a fan club, Holly," Erin Marseille said, fresh from today's last trip between band office and school. "Rosalee, good to see you. Is there room for one more woman in this van of amazons?"

"There's always room for you, Erin," Rosalee said. "Get in, sit down, shut up, and hang on."

"Get me there and back in one piece, you gear jammer."

"You'll have to find your own ride back, sweetheart," Holly said. "Rosalee and I are staying overnight. The bright lights of the city call to us Nemiah girls."

"That's fine with me," Erin replied. "I brought an overnight bag just in case." "I'll stay with my sister." She went to her car to fetch her bag.

"It's nice travelling with Erin," Rosalee said. "She never keeps you waiting. She might also buy us lunch."

"Maybe at Dairy Queen," Holly quipped. "Felix, have my seat. Elders ride in front."

"To suffer more if Rosalee crashes?" Felix asked playfully.

"I won't crash, Felix. I'll get you there in one piece, mostly because I want to get there in one piece."

"As for Dairy Queen, Holly," Rosalee pronounced toward the rear seat, "I'm never going back there. They treat you right, as they say, but I belong behind the wheel. We're going to take over the Cariboo wood industry. Remember?"

"Let's go," Erin said, setting her bag on the seat behind Felix.

People cheered as the van went down the hill from the school and toward the highway.

———

The Anaham school gym was packed with locals, Chilcotins from other communities, and non-Chilcotins from as far away as Ocean Falls, on an island along the coast west of Bella Coola. They had revived the abandoned pulp and paper mill that had once made the town boom. Argentines versed in factory takeover had helped them make it legal. Now the mill operated again, sustainably.

The Heilstuk had brought oolichan, an oily fish with a historic pedigree. It was the reason for the name of the Grease Trail, which ran from Bella Coola to Quesnel. This ancestral trading route, now a wilderness preserve and tourist trail, was how Scottish explorer Alexander Mackenzie got to the Pacific Ocean in 1793, the first man to cross North America by land. A rock in Bella Coola said so. Rocks don't lie. Chilcotins mostly preferred salmon, but some liked the slippery little oolichan.

Some Shuswaps were there, too, including victors from the TransCanada Highway blockade east of Kamloops. The brave Neskonlith people had been saying for years that they didn't want the highway expanded, didn't want to lose more of their land. The provincial and federal governments had offered compensation, but some things shouldn't be commodified, nor valued in money. The residential school Common Experience Payments had proven that: money can't buy away grief.

Money couldn't buy away land either, the settler governments had discovered.

When contractors had tried to bulldoze, literally, their way to expanding the highway, the Neskonlith stood up, with help. Some Blackfoots from Southern Alberta were there, still mourning their sacred Oldman River, mangled by the Three Valleys Gap Dam a generation earlier. A battle of injunctions had ended in Neskonlith's favor, thanks partly to Bruce Culloden's precedent overturning the injunctions against the Fish Lake Road blockade.

The Carrier from Kluskus had brought a whole moose two days earlier. They had dried some and cooked some. Not lazy at all, those Kluskus people. They had come on the all-weather road that now linked Kluskus with Highway 20, just west of Alexis Creek. Roads, health, and now government were shifting west, from the Quesnel-Williams Lake area to traditional Chilcotin territory. Things were returning to what they had been before gold fever had infected Europeans and USians, their feet had trod unceded Chilcotin land, their diseases had killed most Chilcotins, and their institutions had sat on the survivors.

Throw the bosses off your back.

Cara Marseille took the microphone.

"Welcome, everyone. I see that the food is ready. Let's eat, then talk."

Smart chief, that Cara, Albert thought, as he watched the young people line up to get plates of food for the elders. In a few minutes, Randy brought Sarah's and his own plates.

Eating unites people. Breaking bread is older than bread itself. Cook together. Eat together. Talk together. Stand together. The gym felt like something old was about to give birth to something new.

People don't always know when they are living in the midst of historic events. These people knew. They remembered who they were, through the seven generations of outsiders and their paid local henchmen trying to erase those memories, that identity. Now it was the eight generation, the generation that would turn things around. Not return them to some bucolic era that never was; turn them around from injustice to justice, from racism to acceptance, from inequality of edict to equality of outcome. They would go forward, the people united, working for one another, not fractured and made fractious by divisions of race, by settler governments and their schools, by settler businesses and their inequality. The settlers could stay, but on Chilcotin terms, as it should have been in 1864.

"Now that we're fed, let's stop being fed up," Cara began, as the crowd hushed. A few chuckled. Humor sure gets people's attention, Cara thought.

"I'd like to welcome Chilcotins from here and elsewhere, other Indians, and settlers to today's meeting. I hope you ate lots, because we might be here for awhile. Don't worry, though. Nobody leaves a Chilcotin table hungry. There's always a last piece of food for someone. It's our way."

"First, I'd like to congratulate the Nemiah people for stopping mining at Fish Lake. For years, it seemed that mine would never go away. Environmental assessments would damn it. We would block it. Even a government turned it down, although another government approved it, despite a damning environmental report. Years later, there was still no mine, but the threat remained."

"Today that threat is finally dead."

A huge cheer went up from the crowd.

"Thank you, Nemiah, and your many helpers, including people from my community of Anaham."

"There's other good news. Neskonlith protected their land from highway expansion. In Alberta, a major battle continues to stop the tarsands. I think there are a few Alberta Indians here today. I know there are a few people from Ocean Falls here, today. We'll hear from them later. They have some suggestions for our forest industry."

"It's our forest industry, finally!" someone shouted, and many applauded in agreement.

"I won't talk for long," Cara said. A smart alecky cheer went up. "Very funny."

"Seriously, though, I only wanted to relay news from elsewhere, and add some from here. Then I'll turn the mike over to Ocean Falls, then Neskonlith, then anyone else who wants to talk. After that, we'll elect a regional government. That's what I want to talk about now, briefly."

"The Cariboo Regional District is dead." A few cheers.

"The provincial government is will soon be dead, too." Many cheers.

"What about Ottawa?" someone asked.

"We'll see," Cara said, "but we'll have a say in that, too, through the government we'll create here today."

"This is our land. Courts had finally agreed. We knew it all along. Today we will elect one person to represent the Cariboo Chilcotin in an upcoming constitutional conference in Ottawa. Right now in Williams Lake, there is a gathering in the biggest gym in town to do the same for the Cariboo-Kamloops area. Like us, they send a person to Ottawa. This system is based on the size of land, not the size of population."

"It was always about land. Now others understand that."

"Before we elect our constitutional delegate, I would like to hear from Sarah David from Nemiah, Richard Owen from Ocean Falls, and Wanda Patrick from Neskonlith."

A cheer went up. Young people chanted, "Sar-ah! Sar-ah! Sar-ah!"

Randy wheeled Sarah to the microphone stand. As she held the microphone to her mouth, you could have heard a pin drop in the gym, despite the several hundred people there, and double that outside, listening to speakers humming in the crisp fall air.

"Thank you all," Sarah began. "I'm happy to be here. At my age, I'm happy to be anywhere." Laughter from around the gym.

"We stopped the mine, finally; but we didn't do it alone. Now we can make a new, fairer world. I don't know if I'll see that world, but I know that many young people will work together to bring it to be."

Young faces shone as young ears hung on Sarah's every word. We need more Sarahs, Cara thought.

"I won't tell you who to send to Ottawa. I will only suggest that, whoever goes, they remember where they come from. You young people. Keep standing together. Trust one another. You are our future. That's serious business. It can also be fun. That roadblock was fun for me."

Strange idea of fun, Cara thought. She could have been blown up, had the police tried to cut the chains that tied her to those propane tanks. Will I have Sarah's guts, when the time comes? Cara wondered.

"Thanks for listening to this old lady," Sarah ended. Cheers rose from the multitudes inside and outside the gym.

"Thanks, Sarah. I hope I'm as brave as you, when I need to be," Cara said after Sarah returned the microphone. "Now we'll hear from Wanda Patrick from Neskonlith."

Wanda Patrick was younger than Sarah, but older than Cara. She strode onto the stage like someone comfortable and courageous in her skin, a rarity for a Shuswap among Chilcotins.

"Hello, everyone. Thanks for having me here," Wanda began. "Good work, Sarah, and all who helped you stop that mine. As you know, we had a little fight about a highway."

Understatement. RCMP in armored vehicles. Shots fired. People wounded. None killed, luckily. Bulldozers disabled. A media circus. Hamstrung provincial government, its erratic reactions proving its uselessness. Only when Ottawa sent soldiers from Chilliwack, to protect a national highway, did the police provocations stop. The RCMP proved that it was not only useless, but dangerous.

"We only intended to stop TransCanada Highway expansion onto more of our territory than the highway covers now," Wanda explained. "But by the time we won on the blockade and in court, we made the Ottawa government think."

"Good trick!" someone shouted.

"Prime Minister Knight was already thinking of holding some sort of national conference about aboriginal rights and title, but now the future of the RCMP and provincial governments will probably be part of the conference. And it will be a constitutional conference. That means it will change how government works in Canada. It will probably give us more say."

"Government doesn't work in Canada!" someone shouted.

"You're right," Wanda said, a lawyer wanting to overturn laws, or at least laws that held Indians down for generations, for centuries elsewhere in Canada, and the Americas in general. "We need new laws, better laws, laws for all people, not only for the rich. New laws will bring new courts, which will serve us better than the old courts."

"I understand there will be 49 people at this constitutional conference," Wanda continued. "Your region will send one. All together, British Columbia will send ten people, although at the end of the conference there will probably be no more British Columbia. Provincial government will probably be abolished."

"Good riddance!" a voice yelled.

"Why 49 people? Why not 50?" another voice.

"I agree with abolishing provinces," Wanda said. "Why not 100 people at the constitutional conference? That's a good question. I said that BC would send ten people: one from the Chilcotin, one from the Thompson, one Okanagan, one Kootenays, one Northwest, one Prince George-Carrier, one Peace River region, one Vancouver Island, one Vancouver, one Lower Mainland. Notice that Vancouver, with more than a million people, will send one, as you will, and fewer than 100 000 live in your area. This system will represent land as well as population."

"I'm getting to the 49 part," Wanda said, to keep the crowd's interest.

Ten from BC, ten from the Prairie provinces, one Yukon, one Northwest Territories, one Nunavut, ten Ontario, ten Quebec, six Maritimes and Newfoundland. That's 49 in all. Number 50 will come from the United Nations. The U.N. will send a delegate to each country that holds a conference such as ours. The U.N. will be the world government some have always envisioned, but power will be at the bottom, in the regions, not at the top. The U.N. will coordinate, not dictate; although it will have the strongest army in the world, an army populated and paid for by the regions. This army will probably shrink over time."

"We need new government for new times," Wanda said.

Cheers.

"We also need police," she continued.

Boo's.

"No, listen. We had police in pre-contact days. We had people who would enforce proper behavior, behavior upon which our ancestors depended for life and death."

"If someone stole food, or tools, or weapons from the people, the people suffered. If someone became too bossy, the people suffered. There had to be a way to control those who would wreck it for everyone. That won't change until there is a change in the human heart."

"Someday!" a voice rang out, a prophet of a better time coming in human evolution.

"Well, that's all I want to say. Any questions?"

"Will you go to Ottawa and talk for us?" someone asked.

"Send a Chilcotin. This is Chilcotin land. I'm from Kamloops, Shuswap land," Wanda replied. "Perhaps Kamloops will send me, but this constitutional conference needs others besides lawyers."

Albert liked to hear that. A lawyer inviting others into the making of law. A humble lawyer, one without all the answers, for a change. He wondered if his band's lawyer Bruce knew this lawyer Wanda.

A pause. "Any other questions?" Wanda asked. "No? Well then, I'll hand the microphone back to Cara. Thanks for listening to me, everybody."

"Now we'll hear from Richard Owen," Cara said, handing the microphone to a sturdy white man in work clothes. Richard Owen traced his ancestry to his Scottish namesake, Robert Owen, whose early-1800s socialist movement rocked capitalism. Capitalism had endured shocks aplenty since that failed attempt, but it recovered more slowly, and with more authoritarianism, from each shock. Now sounded capitalism's death knell, finally. Richard would build on his ancestor's legacy. A long time woodworker, he had put teeth in a tired, tripartitist, tottering union, then helped replace it with a vigorous, militant, durable union.

Some old things, like tripartite unions, become useless and die. Management, government, and unions are in conflict, two against one; but now unions were becoming management, and people were becoming government. Some old people, like Sarah, get more useful with age. Richard Owen had old ideas from his Scottish ancestors, but these ideas had new power. What a time to live!

"Good day, everyone," he sparked the crowd's attention with his booming voice. "I'm here to tell you how to run your own industry. We do it in Ocean Falls. You can do it here."

"You might know about the mill that closed in our island home years ago. It stayed there while many of us moved away. I moved away for awhile, but I came back last year. People were sick of moving to work elsewhere, when a perfectly good mill sat idle right in Ocean Falls. At one time, hundreds worked there and thousands of people in families up and down the coast prospered."

"I'm happy to announce that good times are back, in Ocean Falls, thanks to our unity, and a little outside help," Richard continued. "People in Argentina have been taking over idle factories for years. A few of them came to Ocean Falls and explained how we could take over that mill. We made it ours. Canadian laws were a challenge, but I'm here today to say that we can change those laws. Meanwhile, you all can get started on running the forestry and mining industries that are on your land."

"We booted out the miners!" someone shouted.

"Yes you did," Richard replied. "You booted out a mining company that wanted to make an unsustainable mine."

We bankrupted it, in effect, Albert thought. Did this Richard Owen want us to dig up our land?

"I don't want you to wreck your land," Richard seemed to read Albert's mind. "We run the Ocean Falls mill in a sustainable way. We don't just make logs into rolls of newsprint and care nothing for our future. We want our children to have jobs in that industry. That's why we use paper to publish books. The Heiltsuk people tell their stories to the world. Heck, even I'm writing a book."

"We also use wood for local housing, and housing along the coast. We get more jobs from one log than the old mill got from ten logs. The Argentines ran factories, not paper mills, but some things they told us helped us. I'm sure they have useful things to tell you."

"We're listening," came from the crowd.

"Forestry is less destructive than mining," Richard said. "I won't lie to you. Still, the world wants your minerals. You can get at them without wrecking your water or fish. You can get the jobs. You can get the profits. Other places are doing it already, places that have thrown out Canadian mining companies like you threw out Dream Metals."

"I'm not a miner, but a Chilean who came with the Argentines to Ocean Falls was a miner. You might know that Chile booted out all the foreign mining companies and nationalized their assets without compensation."

That was a lovely story, a historical wrong righted. The Salvador Allende Movement had gathered strength for years. Named after the Chilean doctor who became president in 1970, the Movement became the government in a landslide election. It kept its campaign promise and nationalized the mines. Allende had died in a hail of bullets from a US-backed coup in 1973.

This time, the US military was so overstretched around the world that it couldn't spare a bullet, let alone an advisor, to foist another coup on Chile when the government nationalized the mines a year ago. Very few in the army wanted a coup, unlike in 1973.

Manifest Destiny, the idea that the entire Americas would fall into the US orbit, and the Monroe Doctrine, the idea that the US should run the Americas, were as dead as mining dividends.

"I recommend you invite that Chilean miner here to advise you on sustainable mining. It's rare, but possible," Richard concluded. "I know more about forestry. Others in Ocean Falls and elsewhere know all sorts of industry that might be possible here, as it is there. We're on an island and we manage. Think of what you can do, with all-weather roads."

"The keys are unity and honesty. Let everyone have a say, as you're doing here today. Hang together or hang separately. Thanks for listening to me. I'll be over by the bannock table if anyone wants to talk more."

Bannock, a Scottish word, attracted a candid descendant of canny Scots.

———

"Hello, Holly. Thanks for coming," Carl Schultz said, bounding to the side of the women's truck outside the local hockey rink. "Who'd you bring?"

"Rosalee Iqallie, this is Carl Schultz. Rosalee drove a logging truck until her mill shut down. Carl is the local union secretary. Carl, we brought a couple other people here, but we dropped them off before we got here. I tell you that because you might think we're pressed for time and must drive them back; but they have places to stay overnight after their business here is done."

Rosalee remembered the animated conversation they had had with Erin Marseille and Peter Poznan coming into Williams Lake. Erin, on board since Anaham, was nobody's fool, and 20 years older and wiser than Rosalee and Holly. She was going to see her sister Mary. A social work professor, Mary Gaston directed the newly-formed People's Network, of government, indigenous, and private social work agencies, but the last were fading fast, finally. People saw privatization for the inefficient, expensive con it was. Luckily, there would be enough public work for the staff of the private agencies, refugees from wrong-headedness, free from a failed "pay the rich" scheme. Anaham Addictions Counsellor Erin had chaffed at being in a university class taught by her younger sister, but when she saw "an old head on young shoulders," she started listening.

Erin had lots to say coming from Anaham to Toosey, though; but she also listened to the younger women. Her main concern had been her brother-in-law, still in Indonesia. Her younger sister's husband had risen in her estimation and she worried about him. What drew him to the Straits of, of where? Moluch? Malaga? Ma-what? It seems that he had been invited there, halfway around the world. Mary would explain, in her patient, gentle, persuasive way.

When the three women had reached Toosey and Chief Peter Poznan climbed aboard, the conversation had taken another, if related, turn. Poznan's Polish name came from the Polish settlers who had come to his land after the 1864 British Army invasion, a century before the more peaceful British Beatles musical invasion of America. But Peter Poznan was Chilcotin, well aware that his people needed him now, and he needed them. He was going to what could become a lion's den: the Williams Lake meeting that would re-organize the school district along progressive lines. That was long overdue and Peter was eager to remind the nervous schoolcrats that more than a quarter of their students were indigenous: real service, no more lip service, Peter intended. Peter lived in the country, but he knew about the world, even about the Strait of Malacca, and why James was there.

―――

"Walter!"
"Hello, Rosalee."
"What are you doing here?"
"They might need a welder. I haven't had a drink in five days."
"That's good news."
"I'm sorry I left you when you lost your trucking job, Rosalee."
"Where are you staying?"
"With Vince at the Jamboree."

People still called it the Jamboree, although it was no longer a motel and had a new name and purpose. The local social housing network had bought the motel when its owners had wanted to sell the money-losing proposition. Now it was a social housing place for single adults, many street people among them. Some rooms had two, even three, people in them, but only temporarily, until people moved to other places. Other places were coming onto the public housing market fast, as other motels and some apartment buildings became public housing.

At centre ice, Carl Schultz had begun talking about the takeover of the last operating mill in Williams Lake.

"I'm so glad to see you, Walter. I'm so glad you're clean," Rosalee said, a thoughtful look on her face.

"The company is bankrupt. The Royal Bank called its loans before the bank went bankrupt," Schultz began. "The union has made an offer to take over the mill. The company will probably accept it. The credit union has agreed to back us. It's not bankrupt. It didn't have overseas investments to drag it down when they went bad. In fact, the credit union is expanding, here and elsewhere. The credit union had to be a conservative lender. It didn't lend to many of you when banks would lend to you, but it didn't have a cushion of cushy overseas money, unlike banks."

"We'll own a mill, perhaps another in a few months. We'll run the show."
Cheers.
"When?" a voice shouted.
"Today or tomorrow," Schultz replied. "We'll need to vote on whether or not to take the mill."
"Take the mill!" a shout.
"I agree," Schultz said. "I hope you all know that it'll cost each one of the union's members money, and free labor for awhile. It'll also cost the new members we expect to sign up. We'll need many new members because we're going to run things differently from how the company ran them. Under us, the place will make more money because it will have more value-added. No more raw logs on trains leaving town."
Cheers.
Walter looked at Rosalee. "I'll probably hire on. They'll need welders to fix the equipment that the company let run down. The trucks from the bankrupt contractors will need repair, too. They never did maintain them properly. Now the union will run the trucks, and keep them running well, so they last. No more tax breaks for run-down equipment that has killed more than one trucker on the road."

"No kidding," Rosalee said. "You remember a couple close calls I had because of crappy truck maintenance. I even had to jump out of a truck on a runaway lane once, when its brakes failed. That was a fright, all right."
"I remember," Walter said. " They'll need more truckers, too. Many of the truckers left town as the company cut back before bankruptcy."
"That's why I'm here, Spark."
She called me by my old nickname, Walter thought. I might get more than a welding job today. Maybe she'll take me back.
"Where are you planning to live, Walter?"
"Many apartment buildings are becoming co-ops. All the buildings of the city's main landlord, and a few others. The landlords are getting out before the people throw them out," Walter said. "They'll have to live like the rest of us, not off the rest of us."
"Vince and I will find something, unless you have another idea."

"I have another idea, Walter. Let's try again. It would be good for Leon, too. Have you seen him lately?"

Their son had shunned his father from the time Walter hit the streets until two days ago. Walter had shown up at the school career fair, clean and sober. Leon was wary, as were Rosalee's cousin's family, with whom he boarded for high school. The two had talked frankly for an hour in the warm fall sun outside the high school.

"I saw him yesterday and apologized for being such an embarrassment for so many months. He's like his mother, doesn't mince words. There's no doubt where he stands, on me, on school, on architecture, of all things. I think we're good again."

Rosalee sighed in relief. Her cousins hadn't said anything about this apparent reunion. They were still sizzled at Walter for leaving Rosalee when she lost her trucking job. They never liked Walter much, anyway.

"Boy, am I glad you're sober and back, Spark. Our son the architect, eh? He tells me there's lots of jobs in that, and he wanted to train in Ottawa, of all places."

"Yeah, he told me, too. He said Carleton University has an architecture program. It's expanding because of the social housing going up everywhere. Perhaps Leon will make houses with the wood you haul, using the machinery I weld."

"Family business, eh, Walter?"

"Yep, a family business, Gears."

Gears, Walter's pet name for me, Rosalee thought, and sighed again.

On stage, Carl was calling for the vote, as if anyone doubted that the hundreds of people in the rink would vote to take over the mill. A half hour later, he announced the results.

"In favor of taking over the mill, one thousand, four hundred and twenty-seven. Opposed, thirteen."

Laughter. Only thirteen opposed! Probably a few old guys from the old union, with old ideas that workers can't run sawmills.

"Thanks for the overwhelming support, brothers and sister," Carl continued. "This will cost us each some money and some free labor, but our jobs will be more secure. For the first time in awhile, there'll be new hires."

Cheers. There were more than 2 000 people packed into the rink bleachers, on floor seating, standing at both ends of the rink, and standing above the bleachers. All these people, many of them skilled and useful to the new mill, as they would have been useful to the old mill, had the company put people before profits. But that's not in capitalism's nature.

As environments change, some organisms thrive and increase their numbers. Others do not thrive, and their numbers decline to extinction. Natural selection favors the well-adapted. Now the economic environment was changing rapidly, favoring those who would work together for all, not alone for profit, their own or their bosses'. Group selection had favored hunter-gatherers who worked together, food-growers who worked together.

The theory of evolution, natural selection its elegant explanation of change over time within species, and the appearance of new species, arose in the mid-1800s. The inefficient, selfish economic system of the time distorted that theory to justify the greed of the strong and the starvation of the weak. Arthur Wallace and Charles Darwin, who first explained evolution, were men of their Victorian English times. Even had they sublimated themselves above the harsh social theories that rationalized poverty among plenty, using their theory, they could not have convinced their world that cooperation, not competition, drove evolution. Even before the recent and definitive crash of capitalism, however, evolutionary theorists elevated the power of groups, of cooperation, in the theory.

The multitude in this hockey rink descended from the groups that thrived over human evolution's few million years, most of those years shrouded in prehistoric mystery. This group's vote proved that people could work for all, and that centuries of greed had been impositions on, not natural to humans. New economic and social conditions favored people ready to work together for all, while those who worked for their own benefit against all would fade to extinction.

Fortune favors the prepared mind, but this fortune would be a shared fortune in a peaceful worked. It would not be a fortune stolen from the few by the many, and defended by private property laws, laws of the thieves of public labor and property. The violence of a state run by the few would give way to the peace of a state run by all. Private property had brought class divisions and war for centuries, for millennia. Public property united people and made war as unlikely as the return of a species that had shown itself unfit to live in the world.

"Thank you all for coming," Carl Schultz concluded. "The tables at the front have sign-up sheets for maintenance, operations, finance, public relations, safety, and lots else. There's also a hiring area off to the side there. Bring your trades papers and you'll probably get a job, but not like a job in the old days, when you put in your time, and go home and forget about it. You bunch will work harder, but work for yourselves and this community, not for financial speculators and their toadies, here and elsewhere."

"This is our mill. Let's run it our way, for ourselves and for our community." Cheers.

"I'm going down to the hiring table, Walter. Wanna come?"

"Does a bear shit in the woods, Rosalee? Damn right I wanna come."

Holly watched the two become one again, one love, one will, one dream. She thought about Randy.

Chapter 6   Tanks to Transit

The United States military had run out of gas, long after it had run out of goodwill, overseas and at home. Now it was going home. That part of President McKay's speech found mass acceptance, especially from war-poisoned veterans, their families, and their communities, tired of sacrificing themselves and their budgets for foreign wars and domestic repression. There was so much retooling to do that even military contractors would be busy, but for peace, at home and abroad.

"Can one make a tank into a commuter rail car? McKay pondered after her speech. "Will the United States become, for the world, "the city on the hill," the ideal state that some of its political pioneers envisioned? What times to be alive!"

    She had worried about this defanging of the military monster more than about the overtly socialist direction which her speech proposed for the United States economy. It seems that her gamble had won: almost all potential opponents rallied behind her, lest the restless millions do worse to the military and corporate rulers now dethroned from their monarchic position atop the republic.

   Even before her speech, some of the army and most of the navy had mutinied, not against her, but against their hidebound leadership. She knew she had the numbers to support her if it came to a civil war, but last night's speech helped prevent a civil war. The air force was a question, but planes need somewhere to land, and the army was strong enough to control rebellious air bases.

    Thank goodness that the soldiers who seized the Colorado and Seattle nuclear facilities wanted peace, not some rapturous end of the world. Make a heaven on Earth, rather than blow up Earth and hope for a heavenly reward in some unproven hereafter. Like her, these soldiers operated on the physical fact of evidence, not on the dangerous fallacy of faith. She could depend on her military, she sighed in relief. She could even depend on it to shrink, as its many brains and machines turned away from death and toward life, for her people and the world.

   Winona McKay was still amazed that the United States' archaic electoral college system had vaulted her, an avowed atheist, into the presidency. That pseudo-democratic electoral college system had to go, her speech announced, in favor of proportional representation.

   The American Revolution had produced a country more democratic than the European despotism of the late eighteenth century, but her country had stood still and therefore fallen behind Europe's and the world's democratic trends since then. A constitutional amendment for proportional representation would be incidental compared with making the republic a real republic, of the people, by the people, and for the people. That would be a big job, albeit aided by the financial and ideological bankruptcy of the ruling class.

   Can tank metal become commuter railcar or bus metal? That was the challenge for engineers from the military and auto industries. The latter had just gone bankrupt once too often for government bailout. They were not at all too large to fail. The citizenry wouldn't stand for a bailout. Instead, her government would take the advice of the old but still sharp Ralph Nader, and buy General

Motors, plants, dealers, and overseas assets, for three billion. The government would pick up Daimler Chrysler's United States assets for a billion, and expropriate Ford, which had refused to open its books to government auditors after its bankruptcy: too many Nazi links there.

All the people and plant could retool the returning military machinery, and people, for constructive rather than destructive purposes. Decades after the failed promise at the end of the Cold War, the peace dividend was arriving.

In Ohio, Pennsylvania, Ontario, Nova Scotia, and Saskatchewan, laid-off steelworkers were going to mills abandoned by US X when it collapsed.

What kind of steel-producing name was USX?

Skilled and unskilled trades people were cleaning their mills, fixing and testing equipment in their mills, and preparing to run their mills. Their mills. Their mills would convert the steel from returning military vehicles into the steel that would make buses, trains, high-speed rails, bridge girders, and many other useful things, for themselves and many other people, none of them finance capitalists looking to make money at the expense of social progress.

Blast furnaces would soon blast again, circumstances and the masses brave enough to exploit them having blasted away the bosses, speculators, and others who gambled with people's futures. This was a sure thing.

———

The United States military wasn't the only army going home, its missiles between its legs like the tails of defeated dogs. At least the United States military had a unified country to retreat to, unlike the Indian military.

Decades in Kashmir were finally at an end for the largest and longest deployment in Indian since the British wisely fled in the late-1940s. Hundreds of thousands of soldiers, from Kerala and West Bengal and other leftist states in India, had tired of oppressing the Kashmiris.

In the 1940s, the departing British had yoked together incompatible lands to make India, and left out some lands and people that should have been part of India. This ensured generations of discord. When one sees two birds fighting, the expression goes, look nearby for an Englishman, the cause of the fight.

Kashmir had declared its independence before the last Indian boot had left its soil. Not a shot was fired. Neither was a shot fired a week later, when it united with Pakistan, happily free of the military albatross that had dominated it for decades. Millions had flooded the streets to demand civilian government, which had come, and they had stayed to demand something with Kashmir, a new state welcoming the voice of experience from its neighbor. A week later, the two were one.

To the east, across the subcontinent, West and East Bengal has similarly united across what had been an international border. Bengali, the language with the sixth greatest number of speakers in the world, was the language of a new, internationalist country. Bengal, like "Pakimir" to the west, was a secular country.

Finally, peace reigned in the Indian subcontinent, thanks more to people tired of war, religious and otherwise, than to "humanitarian intervention" from abroad. Humanitarian bullets? The desperate American empire and its United Nations toadies had abandoned that ruse, that disguised imperialism.

Hinduism and Islam left government and returned to temple and mosque, left the gilt of gold and guilt of violence, and returned to the Golden Rule. As in the US, religion was declining noticeably as people saw that they could improve this world, rather than endure an unjust here for a just hereafter. Religion, "the opium of the masses," was losing its addictive power.

No longer ridden by the rich, nor bamboozled by the righteous, people around the world were setting their own direction, for their good and for the good of the Earth, their long-suffering host.

Earth breathed easier with less fossil fuel consumption. The US military had guzzled a quarter of that country's oil. Now that the war machine was quiet, there was more oil for peaceful uses. More importantly, there was enough oil for the transition to a post-carbon world, before the world warmed too much for anything other than humanity's transition to extinction.

War, that curse born of private property, was no more, as private property was becoming a relic of a long, barbaric era in human evolution. The ape whose brain and thumb had catapulted him above other species, above Earth, above humility, had looked over the brink of that doomed path and pulled back just in time. That thumb, that brain, would serve all people and the Earth now, not enslave people and sabotage the Earth.

Even that tragic territory known as the Eastern Mediterranean was coming to know a peace that passeth centuries of misunderstanding. With oil demand slumped by peace, sand dune despotism blew away in the storms of protests by nationals and foreign workers. Bahrain, Qatar, Kuwait, saw freedom, finally, with minimal bloodshed in its purchase. A few rogue paramilitary outfits faced a stare-down by wiser soldiers and politicians, lest blood drown all combatants.

From Tahrir Square in the west, in Cairo, Egypt to Tarjish Square in Tehran, Iran, people gathered peacefully, but with steely determination that the steel weapons of despots couldn't defeat. Despots rarely opposed, at last, seeing that despotism had had its day. The Nassar Movement in Egypt, the Mossadegh Movement in Iran, and many movements long submerged under imposed divisions of religion and class, tamed religion and transcended class.

Palestine freed itself, with surprising help from Jews, themselves tired of living in the police state known as Israel, illegal since its 1948 imposition on Palestine by conniving, anti-Semitic gentiles and combative Jews in Europe and America. Hundreds of thousands of Jews had demonstrated until the settler colonialist Israeli government peacefully stepped down, before it was dragged down. Zionist no more, not even Bundist, Israel was a loud but brief historical curiosity.

Israel's nuclear weapons joined Pakistan's, under United Nations regulation, which Albert Einstein had advised for all nuclear weapons. The United Nations had rescinded the permanent member status and veto power of the five largest arms traders in the world: the US, Russia, Britain, France, and China. A newly-confident General Assembly had pried loose the nuclear weapons of even these countries. US President McKay secretly thanked the Colorado mutineers for anticipating this world peace by seizing control of their missile silos.

Civilized at last, thanks to its many wise Jews, and millions of wise Arabs surrounding them, Israel was no longer a country, but no longer a battleground. Now, Jews could live as safely as they had lived for centuries before 1948, in cities such as Tehran, Cairo, and Damascus. A few rogues excepted, Israeli military and diplomatic people overseas were coming home, to enjoy reconciliation, not endure recrimination.

Domestic and Diaspora Palestinians had reclaimed a land their ancestors had inhabited for centuries before bullets and lies had stolen it from them in 1940s and later acts of aggression, acts of genocidal intent. Jews who wanted to live, who mourned their ancestors killed by Nazi gas during World War Two, decided to live with Palestinians, not live in engineered fear of Palestinians.

A leap of faith by both sides, faith in the goodness of people, not faith in some divisive religion, had made one state. Bigger than Eretz Israel, this state was secular, not religious, multinational, not nationalist, and stretched from the Mediterranean to the Turkish border. All Jordan, Lebanon, and much of Syria joined the idealistic new venture.

Turkey had dismantled its military rather than continue to be a pawn in a deadly global game. The North Atlantic Treaty Alliance lost its sole Muslim country, but Islam hadn't made Turkey peaceful, although Islam preaches peace to those who understand it correctly. Rather, what made Turkey a model of peace and progress was the wisdom born of centuries of international experience, good and bad, centuries before Europeans blasted their way to world domination, so brief, so dangerous, and now fading so fast. Turkey had lost its Ottoman Empire in the mud of World War One, between 1914 and 1918. It had tried then to become a secular modern state, but international sabotage thwarted that effort. Turkish historians and diplomats could teach the United States how to live without an empire.

Calls to prayer attracted millions still, but millions fewer than when religion drove people to deeds despicable to religion's highest ideals. These ideals were always irrationally-based, and therefore potentially dangerous, and therefore a hindrance rather than a help to humanity for millennia. A new millennia was afoot, a millennia materialistic, exalting human potential, in areas as diverse as music and machinery. No longer did human pettiness rule in the name of this or that god invented by some to justify oppressing others.

The "green and pleasant land" that had made an empire on which the sun never set, was now deep in darkness back in the British Isles; but even there, hope shone brighter as equality increased. The philosophical heirs of several William's, Wallace, Godwin, Wordsworth, and Morris, now worked under benevolent Crown Prince William and his sensible father, King Charles III. The prince would not lose his title, but only most of his family's wealth and lands. His father the king would not lose his head, unlike Charles I.

English Prime Minister George Galloway had talked his way from leading the Respect Party, a group that dissented from "Third Way Labor" and back to the socialism of Labor's earlier era, into leading a coalition of socialists and communists that formed the government. Galloway had resisted an effort to abolish the monarchy, in exchange for abolishing the House of Lords. Galloway was old but energetic, and many followers helped this elder statesman of keen-eyed justice. Progressive taxation and a strong public sector were back, with the bonus of a nationalized banking system, run by the post office. Britain repatriated assets hidden in offshore accounts, putting a final nail in the coffin of piracy that began with Frances Drake centuries earlier. What the people sweated for, the people would enjoy.

Galloway had sent advisors to the US and Canada to help them transform their post offices into national banking systems, but Canada, especially, had a strong credit union system "to bank on," and with. Now, England sent help, not harm overseas. Russia had welcomed its pilfered assets back from English banks, as had many countries. What had once been "the workshop of the world" was now offering hard-gotten wisdom to the world.

Europe in general was humbly rejoining a world that it and the US no longer controlled. France withdrew its soldiers and miners from Africa, Germany its industrialists from South America, Norway its fish farms from Canada. Birth rates were still so low that population decline would ease pressure on the environment and on the poor. European anti-immigrant sentiment transformed into a warm welcome for immigrants, as national workforces aged. The Muslim call to prayer in Denmark no longer met hostility from reactionaries. It helped that religious numbers and power were in steep decline in Europe. Vagaries of faith were giving way to hope, to charity, to action.

Even the Vatican opened its vaults and archives, blood-soaked testimony to the Catholic church's feudal roots; but even there, reconciliation trumped recrimination. Italy welcomed the Vatican back, almost a century after the Italian fascist Mussolini preposterously made a theocratic state of those few square kilometres of Rome.

———

Canadian soldiers, unwelcome in Haiti, Guatemala, Congo, and other places where they tired of thugging for mining companies, took the hint en masse and were returning to Canada. Perhaps there would be useful work for them, for a change. Indeed, a few stayed in other countries to listen and help, rather than dictate and harm.

Quebec soldiers sided with Quebec people. Neither would soldiers from Petawawa, Ontario quell demonstrations in Toronto, Ottawa, or elsewhere. Cornwallis soldiers largely demobilized and went home.

The poverty draft had failed in at least two ways. First, it attracted poor young men and women who profited little or none at all from the way things were. How strongly would they defend a system that fed upon them rather than fed them? Not strongly, it turned out. Second, an army of people fleeing poverty did not listen to career officers, indeed convinced some of them to lead a people's army, not an army bludgeoning the poor, here and elsewhere, for the rich.

At Canada's western tip, the Esquimalt Naval Base, an argument ensued that was similar to arguments at military bases across the country, and beyond. Commanding Admiral Arthur Douglas had heeded the advice of his subordinates and parked his fleet, rather than send it to intimidate the newly-declared Vancouver Commune. One subordinate begged to differ.

A former school principal and graduate of the local public university when it was newly-freed from its military heritage, Jude Sterns wanted to fight the commune, wanted to fight the march of history, just wanted to fight. Exposed as a police informant while running the school of a Kootenay Indian band, he could not buy a job in a school: principal, teacher, janitor, nothing. Using his degree and connections from what had been a military university in Victoria, Sterns had gotten an officer's commission. He was a naval lieutenant in Esquimalt.

This commission cost him his long-suffering spouse, who had chosen to return to the Chilcotin rather than follow him from the Kootenays to Esquimalt. A teacher herself, she had grown up ranching near Nemiah. Aline Sterns sympathized with the Chilcotins people more than her reactionary spouse could bear. Aline had returned to Williams Lake, found a teaching job, and attended the local meeting that would send delegates to Kamloops, to decide whom to send to the constitutional conference in Ottawa.

"The masses are stupid. Only emotion and hatred can rule them," Jude had told Admiral Douglas, a distant descendant of Governor Douglas, the master compromiser soon compromised himself, with regard to the first peoples of British Columbia.

"Jude, you're on the wrong side of history, and I studied history, at the same university that graduated you. I am older than you. I have seen active duty off the Guatemalan coast, in Haiti, and in many other places I'm now embarrassed to admit."

"Sir, with all due respect, we must show force in Vancouver, or lose it."

"Lieutenant, with all due respect, we must show peace in Vancouver, or lose our chances of being part of the march of history."

"History marches where the strong direct it, admiral."

"History marches where the wise direct it, lieutenant. Join us in supporting a new, peaceful Canada, that will even have room for such as you."

"Sir, it's against all I believe in, all I was taught, in the local university, and in the hard university of life."

"Jude, you won't betray me. You're too smart to stand apart from great changes, from great chances, for you, too. On sturdy, savvy people such as you, we can build a new world in the shell of the old."

"I don't know, sir. Many among those Vancouver Commune leaders would kill the both of us, if given the chance."

"I agree, Jude. But we're military men, and death is our currency. We might become valuable to men such as those who would kill us. The people are speaking. We can listen and help, or we can resist and fade to irrelevance."

"Well, I do want to contribute any way I can, sir."

"That's the spirit, Jude! Go ashore in Victoria to attend the conference that will choose someone to represent Vancouver Island in the upcoming constitutional conference. Who knows? They might choose you."

Othello trusts Iago. Times were changing indeed.

Jude Sterns' face colored, first with ambition, then with thought. Thought, more than ambition, would rule the new Canada, and the new world.

Jude went home, thought of the estranged Aline, and rested, thoughtfully, in his brother Jerome's Victoria house. At least Jude felt he had a home to go to.

Israeli fighter pilot Avi Levins felt that he had no home to go to, felt that his Israel had been stolen by the people his father and grandfather had wrested it from decades earlier. Deployed in Canada's Cold Lake airbase as part of an international military cooperation scheme that had outlived NATO, Levins coasted north from Cold Lake toward Fort Macmurray. This routing training flight would be anything but, if he had his way, and he was at the controls and would have his way.

NATO, the North Atlantic Treaty Organization, a 1947 military alliance born of US and English paranoia about communism washing up on their shores, had expanded by 2010 to include countries far from the Atlantic shore: Bulgaria and Turkey, for example. After the Warsaw Pact, a military alliance formed in 1955 to tame NATO, had unravelled in the early-1990s, NATO picked up some pieces, some countries that traded membership in one pact for membership in another. Each pact had used more than helped such countries.

Russia had led the Warsaw Pact, and disbanded it in hopes that the US-led NATO would disband; but NATO, that "stinking corpse of the Cold War," had survived, like a zombie whose only purpose was to eat the living to sustain itself. It started as an aggressive, expansionist scheme, like a cancer on the body politic of the world. It had become too expensive, financially and politically, for the US government within the past two years. The military zombie, the tumor, had finally succumbed a few months ago. The world, including the US, had breathed a collective sigh of relief. A mighty parasite had been felled, and green shoots of promise poked through the weary, but still fertile soil.

The Boreal forest, large green shoots, the lungs of the Northern Hemisphere, now ravaged by with clear cuts and tarsands operations, rolled beneath Israeli Captain Levins as he focussed on his target, Highway 63. More precisely, Levins focussed on the Highway 63 Blockade, a sea of people that reminded him of his dad's tales of the retreating Egyptian army in 1973, sitting ducks for Israeli planes. The Russians had convinced the Egyptians to retreat, rather than conquer Israel; but Avi's dad and other pilots had become war criminals by strafing the retreating army.

"Yeah, but Egypt never attacked Israel again," he remembered his father's words. The Zionist one-note historical tune ignored the international diplomatic symphony that had tuned and tamed warmongers on both sides, lest the world ignite for the sake of some scriptural imperative.

Avi unlocked his guns as his plane descended toward Highway 63. In seconds, it was all over, death rained from the sky on a defenceless multitude. Clean, crisp, like a video game, Avi made his statement in blood.

On the ground, chaos reigned. Bertha Janvier, from Fort Chipewyan, felt the wind of the bullets but not the bullets, luckily. Others were not so lucky. Screaming, groaning, dying people lay on the road and in the ditches. This was not death the way it had come to Bertha's sister Paula, death by incremental pollution, death by cancer, creeping up a young woman's body like some industrial molester. This was sudden and sharp.

"Get in the woods! The plane might come back!" Bertha shouted. She ran to help the wounded hide, help the frightened unstuck themselves, save themselves in the Boreal forest that was their ancestral home.

But Avi Levins' plane didn't strafe a second time. Cold Lake had found him, and Wainwright had found Cold Lake.

"Captain Levins, come in. This is Cold Lake calling. Report your location."

"I am just north of the junction of the Clearwater and Athabasca Rivers," Levins calmly replied. Death camp commandants played Bach between gassings. By their emotional detachment, ye shall know the psychopaths.

"Our radar has picked up firing from your area. Anything to report?"

"I did what had to be done."

The radio silence told Levins that Cold Lake was coming after him. Now he could go down in a blaze of glory, a Rapture.

Only a few in Cold Lake knew that Wainwright was coming after them.

"What the hell is going on up there?" Wainwright Canadian Forces Base Commander Ian Helting barked at his attendant corporal.

"We have received reports of a plane, possibly Israeli, firing on the Highway 63 blockade."

"Where does that crazy pilot think he is? Gaza? Who let him up in the air?"

"Cold Lake is looking into it, sir."

"Wainwright is on its way, Corporal. Tell Cold Lake to get it together or we'll do it for them when we get there."

"Yes, sir."

Corporal Max Rosen was one of many in Wainwright who liked the new direction that Canada was taking, a direction toward peace, away from war, toward progress, away from reaction. He would happily relay his commander's words to Cold Lake Airbase.

As he dialed the phone, he heard engines starting outside. This commander commands, he rejoiced. We'll be in Cold Lake by sundown.

Up in Cold Lake, Commander Peter McKinley was going up one side and down the other side of a roomful of officers, most Canadian, some Israeli, a few USian.

"I want the man who let that maniac pilot take off. I can look up who you are, and make it much worse for you, or you can step forward, and possibly save many lives, here and elsewhere."

A timid hand rose from the multitude. "I cleared Levins for takeoff, sir; but he said he was going on routine training flight. You know that we have had these for many years, with no mishaps."

"A rogue pilot, eh?" Commander McKinley pondered aloud. "If the three planes we sent to bring him down bring him down alive, he'll rue the day he met me."

"Wainwright is on its way here. I want no heroes defending this base. We're all in the same Canadian military." Some grumbles from the room.

"I'm not stupid. I know that some of you Israelis and USians have come here because your countries no longer welcome your cowboy carelessness. I don't advise you to incite anything among loyal Canadian pilots. I know some Canadian pilots don't like the direction Canada is taking, but you are outnumbered, in the streets and in the military."

"I expect full cooperation with the Wainwright troops when they arrive. Civil war is for other states, for failed states such as the US and Israel, not for Canada."

Corporal Max Rosen thought to himself, "Here I am, one of the few Canadian Jews on this Wainwright base. I am embarrassed by the rash act of an Israeli Jew. Not one Canadian gentile has threatened to skin me alive, here in redneck southeastern Alberta. Today I am proud of my multicultural country."

Rosen returned to his phone to help coordinate the Wainwright movement to Cold Lake, a manoeuvre larger than any he had ever seen. Corporal Rosen, the carpenter's son from Lethbridge, saw himself as an actor in an historic drama. He was glad he hadn't joined the Israeli Defense Force, as a couple cousins had done. Didn't hear much from them lately; probably in a hot mess in Palestine. Serves them right, for signing up with "the chosen people," against "the people."

Wainwright, Cold Lake, Palestine, Bengal, the people united, never to be defeated, their armies serving them rather than starving them. Bank on a better future.

Chapter 7: Banks Not Made of Marble

When you owe the bank a hundred thousand dollars and you can't pay, you're in trouble. When you owe the bank a hundred million dollars and you can't pay, the bank is in trouble. The banks were in trouble. Red ink flowed through the banks that had seemed "made of marble," that now dissolved like sand.

Canadian banks fell like dominos pushed over by the force of mining companies themselves falling to nationalization, some due to bankruptcy, some due to resistance to mining companies' shadowy practices, in Canada and overseas.

Auto makers, other manufacturers, pharmaceutical, water, food, chemical, computer, health, insurance, and educational service companies, military contractors, retailers including Walmart, the "seven sisters" oil companies, all were bankrupt or about to be bankrupt.

The dreaded $200 barrel of oil profited the oil companies ever so briefly, before it rippled through the world's economy like a financial tidal wave, sweeping most everything before it. Walmart with its warehouses on the highway was, remarkably, one of the first large firms to fold. The business crash reverberated to the oil companies' balance sheets, soon terminally out of balance. Capitalism had made the rope. Capitalism had sold the rope. Capitalism had hung itself by the rope. Governments dare not intervene to reanimate the corpse, with masses of people at government and corporate gates throughout the world.

Instead, governments, and some newly-organized groups of people, seized corporate assets and accounts. Business leaders and their monetary and social henchmen who had misrepresented those assets and accounts went to jail if unrepentant, or offered to help build the new, just world if wise.

Jail wouldn't last long for the incarcerated: the prison-industrial complex was an expensive waste of people and resources, and was winding down. The new world, not a brave new world spoken of by Shakespeare and satirized by Huxley, but a truly new world, of new and happy possibilities, would need these jailbirds to help it soar to heights previously undreamed of: heights of equality, justice, fairness, human potential, so much purer than the private financial heights that once seemed inevitable, but were now extinct. Prison time would be pondering time for the arbitrage cowboys, bucked off into thoughtfulness.

An international system that had been based on trading goods and services had become one that traded currency, options, and futures, had self-destructed in a blizzard of streets full of people and balance sheets empty of value.   If it wouldn't change, then capitalism had no future, critics within and without had warned for years, unheeded. Capitalism had sowed the seeds of its own destruction.

What Sarah David did was not unique. Wherever there are mining companies trying to steal and ruin indigenous land, there are Sarah Davids. Their growing numbers reached a point that tipped over mining companies, made their death squads and government lackeys realize they should switch sides and join their own people. These collaborators knew they would remain after the mining companies fled back to Canada, the country that boasted the most mining head offices in the world. Hollow boast now. The fleeing companies brought seas of red ink that helped crash the Canadian banking system. A old woman in a wheelchair, chained to propane tanks and blocking a mining road was one actor in a wilderness; but many others in many other places resisted in ways this humble, or in ways more elaborate, more dangerous even.

    Like drops of water among mountain rocks, these little acts of resistance were not connected, but the same gravity caused each drop. As drops joined to form trickles, and trickles joined to form streams and rivers, a flood of resistance washed away a centuries-old system that had exploited people and nature. The first Europeans to settle in America came for gold, fur, wood, and other natural treasures in and on a land already inhabited by people. By sword and bible and disease and law, Europeans had killed or bewitched the locals into shunning resistance.

    The gravity of the exploitation had become apparent in America and elsewhere, causing the descendants of those locals and of settlers to bring the weight of the numbers and the measure of their dreams down upon the expropriators. The expropriators were being expropriated, washed away by a peaceful but determined flood, a flood that brought in new ways, humane ways, ecological ways of living.

    Banks floated away like sweepers, trees overhanging a creek, their dominance as shaky as the eroding ground around their roots. The banks were not made of marble, but of dirty deeds, withering under the bright light of public knowledge, of public wrath.

    Banks in the United States, England, and Germany, banks with money so old that few dared to view its damnable sources, were bankrupt. For a few years, currency speculation, derivatives trading, and money laundering had been a financial chewing gum to hold together these houses of cards, but national governments, even where the bank headquarters were, had prohibited such financial slight-of-hand. Thousands, millions of people at the governments' doors had demanded it. There would be no bank bailout this time. The people's money would not build the people's banks.

Indeed, money had changed. In a nationally-televised speech, US President McKay had announced the abolition of the Federal Reserve System, that early-1900s scheme in which banks controlled the US money supply. By the stroke of a pen, banks had been able to create wealth, to destroy wealth, to destroy lives. European and Asian countries had erected central banks that did likewise, on the advice of bankers: cats regulating mice. Finance capitalism couldn't exist forever beside democracy, and the mice had come by their millions to bell the cats. For awhile, it seemed as if finance capital would triumph over democracy that had become a theatrical veneer over a system of bought and sold politicians. Veneer seen through, people such as McKay were in power, and based their power on the people, not on the banks. The brave president with the coal-black hair had stared down the oligarchs and defeated them.

Now she would depend on the many voices of financial reason long hushed by those same oligarchs and their servants in media and government. Like Chicken Little in the fairy tale, the oligarchs had shouted, "The sky is falling! The sky is falling!" but only they and their power fell. The financial sky did not fall. Blue skies, hopeful skies, merely burned through what had been so cloudy for so long that it had seemed normal. When a person is in a stinky room so long that she no longer notices the stink, the newness of fresh air can frighten her, but she soon basks in the clean and pure, finally replacing the dirty and fetid.

President McKay basked in the fresh new world she was helping to create, a cooperative congress and senate agreeing, partly from belief in the new world, partly from belief that these hoary bodies could be helpful and stay relevant; or oppose the progressive trends bursting all around, and land in the dustbin of history.

Welcome to the American Revolution, Part Two.

———

Mike Vidic walked into the Williams Lake and District Credit Union and looked at the big bulletin boards newly installed in the roomy office recently vacated by an investment company recently gone bankrupt. One bulletin board offered advice to the well-heeled whose recently tripped up by the bankruptcy. Another explained the credit union's plans to expand to the Royal Bank and Scotia Bank buildings, their customers its newest members. The main branch, where Mike stood, would handle cooperative and indigenous group financial matters. He looked at the list of staff for the woman overseeing the indigenous side of the operation.

"Jennifer Brant, eh?" Mike said aloud. Off the main lobby, Mike found her door, open, the mutual funds office that had been there gone with the winds of financial change blowing across Canada and the world.

"Ms Brant?" Vidic asked the indigenous woman behind the desk. "I'm Mike Vidic, here on behalf of Nemiah."

"Oh, hello, Mike. I've been wanting to meet you. You're quite famous."

"Huh?"

"It's not every day that a money man for a mine switches sides to work for an Indian band. How do you like is so far?"

"I really like it. I like it more than I liked working for Dream Metals."

"What do you like about this new job, Mike?"

Mike hadn't expected this sort of greeting. There were questions, as there had been in that Vancouver courtroom and children's charity years ago, but these questions relaxed rather than irritated him. No longer was he the resentful street thug buffeted by this or that authority figure. This banker was an authority figure, but not like the social workers and cops who had grilled him, not even like Simon and Johanna van der Waals.

She exuded an authority born of traditions contrary to those of government, police, and business people. It was as if Jennifer Brant had grown authoritative by struggling against, not for such people. This country really had a hidden history, a hidden font of ethics contrary to the one imposed by settlers. Her distant ancestor Joseph Brant had led his people against European encroachment two centuries earlier. Jennifer Brant had a toughness similar to Joseph's.

"For one thing, Ms Brant, my new job will probably be more secure than my last job. Something else, too: I find people trusting me to do more on my own, even if I err, and they are quicker to sympathize and correct me than to chastise me."

"You work for Chilcotins, all right, Mike. Call me Jennifer. I think we'll get along just fine."

"What did I say that makes it obvious to you that I work for Chilcotins, Jennifer?" Mike asked.

"They are a patient people. They let outsiders have great freedom. When those outsiders mess up, Chilcotins might say, 'I told you so,' but they say more strongly, 'We'll give you a second chance.' That makes outsiders who work for them respect Chilcotins more. Nemiah trusts you to be here. Think about that."

"You're not Chilcotin, then?"

"Nope. I'm Six Nations, from Southern Ontario. My people are like Chilcotins in some ways, and unlike them in some ways. Settlers often think Indians are the same across Canada. Settlers who take the time to see differences get along better with Indians."

"Think of yourself, Mike. You're an immigrant, the same color as Greek and Norwegian immigrants, but you're more unlike them than you are like them. The people who understand that are the people with whom you get along better."

"Are you a banker or a psychologist?" Mike blurted out.

"I'm a banker, but I also have good ears, lots of patience, and curiosity about the many different people I meet. I think these habits make me a better banker."

"I wasn't always a banker. I had a tough upbringing, as almost all indigenous people have in Canada. I could have become a criminal, but a few people inspired me to use my brains for socially-useful work."

Her history sounds like mine, Mike thought. We're different, all right, and she explains that well; but she's more like me than those Howe Street bluebloods I endured for the mining company.

"What socially-useful work can I do for you today, Mike?"

"Well, I said I was here for Nemiah. They had their accounts at Royal Bank, but it's gone. I want to move them here. Much of their money is from the federal government, and I want to know how stable that income source is now."

"Mike, don't worry. You're not the first band staffer to come to me concerned about band funds. Nemiah has been pretty careful with its money. The federal government will keep it coming, and probably increase it after the constitutional conference. If you have signing authority, and I assume you have, then you can sign the necessary papers to move the band's accounts here."

"You mean they didn't lose them in the bank crash? I expected worse news than this."

"The news isn't all good, but yes, all the band's Royal funds will come across. The federal government insisted that the bank pay public agencies and individual account holders before it paid private businesses, when the bank failed. Federal auditors were quick to the bank's national headquarters, to troll the books and prevent any funny business. They found many inconsistencies, some of them criminal, in those books. The bank's officers went along with the government insistence, rather than going along to jail."

"That would have been a very interesting financial meeting," Mike noted.

"No kidding. A Six Nations person was at it and told me about it. She was there to remind the government to lean on the bank for the indigenous people. With indigenous power so strong in Canada now, the government readily agreed. The fact that government heeded us felt like more of a triumph than the financial guarantees that resulted, she said, and I agreed."

"Please explain all this to Nemiah when you get back there. I want an open and honest relationship between this credit union and every Indian band it encounters. Mike, you help me and I'll help you."

"No problem, Jennifer."

"Now, it's noon and I'm hungry. I've been here since seven, but I'll get out of here by three, I hope. This afternoon I'll resume training a young man and a young woman from local Indian bands to help me with the Scotiabank and Royal takeovers. These two are sharp, and I want to be sharp. To keep up with these young keeners, I need something to eat. That's why I want to go next door to Sam's Restaurant for lunch. Wanna come?"

"That's the best offer I had all day, Jennifer. I'm there," Mike said, trying to ooze Slavic charm.

This guy's an interesting outsider, Jennifer thought, like me. He gets to the point, like me. And he's easy on the eyes.

"Let's go, then," Jennifer said, the "then" a standard Cariboo ending to a wide variety of sentences.

Outside, the late fall midday sun shone brighter for them both.

"Marcel Dubrovsky?" Prime Minister Knight's secretary asked the aging man with the bright eyes.

"Yes, here as asked," Dubrovsky replied, his voice surprisingly young. "I have an appointment."

"Yes you have," the secretary said. "The prime minister will be happy to see you."

She'll be happy to keep her job, Marcel thought. I'm the one who can help her keep it. Had her ilk listened to me a few years ago, this necessary transition might have been less traumatic. He walked through the open door into the large office of the prime minister, where he never expected to be; but expectations were coming true all over the country, all over the world.

"Professor Dubrovsky, I'm so happy you came. I need you."

Understatement.

"What can I do for you, Madame Prime Minister?"

"My special advisor in economics and tax is over his head lately and I need someone with different skills for different times," Knight replied. "I'll keep him on. Perhaps you can educate him."

The former prime minister in this sinecure special advisor job had been over his head as prime minister, Marcel thought. Now he was swamped, but would he listen? If he wanted to remain useful, it would be in his interest. He had rarely listened to opposing views when prime minister.

"I'll try. What skills of mine do you need?"

"I'll get right to the point. The traditional banking system is finished in Canada, but Canada needs some sort of financial system. I know that you have written extensively on economics and banking. I thought you might have some ideas."

"I'm flattered that you read my writings, Madame Prime Minister. I commend you."

"Don't give me any undue credit, professor. Mostly my ministerial underlings read them and gave me executive summaries. Some of my staff have shown amazing mental flexibility."

"As have you, to invite me here today," Marcel said. The long march through the institutions, which we 1960s idealists began so many decades ago, didn't corrupt us all, it seems. Some kept their ideals. Some passed them on to younger people. There's hope, he thought.

"What do you suggest, in general?" Knight asked.

"A national credit union system with local and regional democratic control," Dubrovsky replied. "You know that Quebec has such a system already, and it is expanding to assume the duties of the failed banks there. It seems to be working, with a few bumps along what is a steep learning curve."

"Could you oversee its implementation nationally? At least we don't need to build any banks. There are plenty. There are also post offices everywhere, and this week I re-opened the many closed ones. The postal unions have agreed to transform them into postal banks. The union came to me about this, but I had been thinking about it already."

This woman is amazingly flexible, Dubrovsky thought. She's smarter than I gave her credit for being. Perhaps the disgrace and departure of the rightist hacks and fools has allowed her to think for herself. I am impressed.

"I like the postal bank idea, Madame Prime Minister. As you know, the Canadian Union of Postal Workers has pretty canny financial wizards."

"I saw that in the last contract negotiations, professor. That's what made me think they'd be useful in banking. What do you say to my offer? Will you help set up a new national banking system?"

"Madame Prime Minister, your offer flatters me, but I am an old man. I do, however, know younger people who would jump at the chance; but I'd stay on to advise, as much as these aging bones would allow."

" I expected that sort of answer, and I also expected you to know younger people who think like you, who could help. It's you I want, but also those you know, whom I and my office don't know. I have been so worried."

Another understatement.

"May I offer a couple suggestions, Madame Prime Minister?"

"I welcome them, professor."

"Well, firstly, the Quebec system renamed itself Caisse des Peuples, "The People's Credit" a fair translation. It had been Caisse Desjardins. Quebec is, arguably, a nation within a nation. It might be politic to let it keep its system, and control over it, while you roll out a parallel system across the rest of Canada."

"I have thought about that, professor," Knight said. "Quebec is indeed a nation within a nation, and I want good relations among the parts of Canada, going into this constitutional conference. You have no doubt heard about the conference."

"I am the delegate from the Outaouais Region, across the river from where we are standing," Dubrovsky replied.

"That is reassuring," Knight said. "Well, there probably won't be a Quebec, probably not be any provinces or provincial governments after this conference, professor; but the millions of Quebecois aren't going anywhere, and they form a distinct society. I plan for the conference results to respect that."

"It will be a more important conference than the 1860s ones that formed Canada, in my view," Dubrovsky said.

"What is your other suggestion, professor?"

"Ensure local control over these financial institutions, control by the citizens, the worker-owned cooperatives that are replacing private businesses, and by the social organizations that are replacing government agencies."

Those social organizations made Knight nervous, but she could not stop their growth. Every day, she wanted less and less to stop them, anyway. Areas as diverse as child welfare, environmental stewardship, and education were being taken over by local groups, large and small, groups with diverse philosophies and plans. Would Canadian unity survive? Knight worried.

Would the Vancouver Commune, in her precious home city, use its ample power and unity to help national unity? She could only hope, and listen to Vancouver's constitutional delegate. She was glad it chose to send a delegate to the upcoming constitutional conference.

"Professor, I couldn't, my government couldn't dictate to local financial operations, large or even small, even if it wanted to. Truly, it no longer wants to. I certainly don't. I am trusting Canadians here, and so far, my trust is justified.

I find myself sleeping easier with each passing day, as I hear news of peaceful transitions in many industries and agencies. This has been a pleasant surprise to me. Not only is local control unstoppable, but I think it is the best way. I sure didn't think so a few months ago, and certainly not when I was British Columbia's premier a few years ago."

"Madam Prime Minister, I commend you for your own transition. You surprise me."

"Professor, I am a politician. I know how to survive in what can be a rough game."

"Thank you for inviting me. I hope I have helped you."

"You have helped more than you might know. Your main help is your link to others whom I don't know, others whom you do know, who can help Canada through this transition and beyond. People, singly and together, make a difference, professor. I always believe that. Now I merely consort with people vastly different from my former acquaintances. I like these new acquaintances more than I expected to like them."

These people I know have been eager, some for years, to see a truly socialist Canada, Dubrovsky thought. Now they will. I never thought I'd see the day. I wish I were 40 years younger. What times we live in!

"Is that all, Madame Prime Minister?"

"That's all for me for now, but please see my secretary on your way out. She wants names of people you recommend to help us, to help Canada. She also wants you to say who can do what, and what importance it has. I'm afraid we're quite at sea lately. I need a better captain, professor."

These people I'll recommend, Dubrovsky thought, these names I'll give, the government already has many of, on its lists of dissidents, some with criminal records from having been arrested at anti-capitalist demonstrations. Won't these former pariahs be surprised to be sitting in the economic catbird seat. I hope they keep true to their leftist slogans. They will, if they remember that people power raised them, and people power can topple them. This is a smart prime minister, conscripting people power to maintain her own position.

Dubrovsky left the room and met a somewhat-nervous but eager prime ministerial secretary, holding a notepad, about to listen to his every word. Dubrovsky gently chuckled and shook his straggly grey locks. He reached into his suit coat's inside pocket for his address book. This government sure wanted that book's precious list of people for other reasons, not so long ago.

Marcel Dubrovsky, Professor of Economics at the University of Ottawa, realized that there was hope. He was glad he had lived so long.

Fifteen minutes later, Prime Minister Knight's secretary nosed in her door and said, "That Dubrovsky you saw today. He gave me his list of people to help with the financial transition."

"I know. I also know that some of them were probably on terrorist watch lists that the former prime minister collected. Did you want to talk about that?"

"No, Amy. I anticipated some of the names. That doesn't bother me. We need all the help we can get. It's something else."

"Yes?"

"As he left, that economist Dubrovksy said, 'You'll need a new kind of money supply, but only temporarily. In a few years, we probably won't need money at all, as we have known it since Sumeria.' Curious statement. What kind of society runs without money? What has Sumeria to do with it? I think that's the ancient name for Iraq, or somewhere around there."

"Did his comment make you nervous, Arlene?"

"Well, Amy, yes it did; but we have little choice but to trust him, right?"

"Right. I think it will work out fine, Arlene. Anything else?"

"No, Amy. If you trust him, then I trust him. I have known you for a long time, and your gambles always worked out. It's just that this is such a big gamble: a new constitution, the abolition of provincial government, all these social organizations replacing bankrupt businesses."

"Arlene, there is a Chinese expression, considered a curse. Many people know the first part of it, 'May you live in interesting times.' The other two parts are, 'May you come to the attention of the authorities' and 'May all your prayers be answered.'"

"You know that our times are interesting, and that new authorities are replacing old authorities, and you might doubt that we have a prayer of surviving this transition; but I see the curse as a prophecy instead. The curse arose in a feudal era, when interesting times likely meant bad times, such as war and famine. Coming to the authorities' attention likely meant jail or execution. Having all your prayers answered presumed that you prayed for sensible, lasting things, not merely wealth or power, which often attract violence from people who would take those away from you."

"Our times are interesting, but in a positive way, I hope, and pray. New authorities now replacing old authorities rely on the power of people, ordinary people, not arms, wealth, or trickery."

"Arlene, if this country has democratic roots, if its people, the powerful and the powerless, believe in the rule of the people, then we have little to fear in this transition. For all my political career until these last few months, I have smiled to cameras and said words put in front of me by rich and powerful people, and those who write for them. That always made me a little uneasy, as if I was lying to people, or at least disconnected from people."

"As voter turnout plunged in the last few elections, I had a growing feeling that this system wasn't serving the majority of Canadians. My majority government got 24% of the vote of eligible voters. That's no majority. That's no mandate to lead the country. People stopped voting when the system stopped reflecting their hopes and dreams, and prayers. Democracy was a mere word, covering a public relations circus every four years, called an election, but more a bamboozle of the public. A shrinking few played along and voted. A majority stopped caring."

"Now it's different. To our political democracy we have added economic democracy. People are taking over factories, corporate farms, media, distribution and retail, everything. People that motivated will want a say in the government. They'll see it as theirs, not a plaything of business, because business, you probably noticed, is in terminal decline."

"I noticed, Amy," Arlene said. "Do you think the voter turnout will increase?"

"Not only will it increase, but it will be a turnout of people who want a government by folks such as themselves, not a government of corporate and legal puppets of lobby groups, as we have now. Look at the current United States election campaign."

"It's pretty fierce, as always."

"Yes, but before it was fierce with attack ads. Now it's fierce with philosophical debate. There are the two main parties, as always, but there are regional parties, and those referendum questions on the national ballot."

Secretary Arlene Mah remembered the gist of the referendum questions. "'Should the United States abolish the electoral college system in favor of a system in which people vote directly for presidential candidates?' 'Should the United States abolish the presidential veto?' 'Should the United States outlaw the sending of U.S. military, private or public, outside the country?' If those questions pass, then the United States will be a very different country."

"I agree, Arlene. I think the questions will pass, and make a more democratic United States. I think our upcoming constitutional conference will make a more democratic Canada."

"Madame Prime Minister, you know that one topic at the conference will the future of the office of prime minister. Are you worried?"

"Not a big, Secretary Mah. I'm eager to see the outcome. I trust Canadians. Left to think for themselves, not herded this way and that by pollsters and pundits and propaganda, I think Canadians do the right thing. The people know the way. What other attitude could a true democrat have?"

This woman, Arlene Mah thought, is a canny one. She knows how to gauge the public wind and tack her political sail accordingly. Amelia Knight left her cushy newscaster job for the knuckly world of British Columbia politics. Behind her winning smile is a wily brain. Mah hoped she could keep up.

The sun was bright in Ottawa that late fall day. Vancouver was overcast, but the two were in the same country still, however little national borders meant anymore. Borders hadn't hindered capital flow, hadn't hindered the rich one percent milking one country and fattening another, or fattening some offshore bank account. The rich had had their day. Now the people were deciding. The offshore banks had been found, their pirated booty returned to those whose labor made it. The World Trade Organization was now the World People's Alliance, headquartered in Shanghai, husbanded along by a Chinese Communist Party that was returning to its roots, and moving away from the slave state it had been, that would have shamed Mao.

The discussion between Canadian Prime Minister Amelia Knight and socialist economist Marcel Dubrovsky was similar to discussions in corridors of power in many places: Washington, Jakarta, Tokyo, Delhi, Moscow, Berlin, London, Johannesburg and Caracas even, their revolutionary socialist governments helping to lead in the world revolution that Trotsky envisioned, without the bloodbath that Lenin imposed on revolutionary Russia a century earlier.

The occupants of those corridors of power had despaired of keeping their power, but most had seen that by enlisting and trusting the millions of people around them, they might be useful to the ongoing revolution. Like Knight, these were politicians, versed in survival in a wide variety of social and economic conditions. Using their ears, they would keep their heads, but not their lavish entourages and expense accounts.

Also like Amy Knight, many world leaders welcomed the transition. Most had entered politics to improve life for their people. Not all had glibly said so to cover their selfish dash for wealth and power. Now they had their chance, undistracted by the self-serving advice of acquaintances there to serve themselves and their rich corporate masters. Artists who bowed to Renaissance popes and princes produced lasting works. Modern courtiers produced the revolution that would topple them, if their pockets continued to rule their sense.

Leaders were finding new acquaintances, as Knight had found Dubrovksy. Leaders always knew of such people because they spied on, jailed, and did worse to such people. Now they needed them. Now they listened to a message vilified by the leaders' former acquaintances, the real enemies of such people, the real enemies of the people.

People just a person by the company she keeps. Canadian Prime Minister Amelia Knight and United States President Winona McKay were changing the company they kept. Canadians and USians noticed, and approved.

Chapter 8: Oil for Peace

"When will James be back, Mary?" Erin asked her sister in Williams Lake.
"I don't know, but I know that he's safe. He's careful."
"Why did he go? Why him, so far away, to where?"

"The Strait of Malacca, in Indonesia, Erin," Mary said.

Mary was patient with her sister's narrow mind. Erin was better than she had been when James and Mary first got together. Neither family liked the match, especially James' family. Their educated white sibling took up with an Indian, but that wasn't what maddened them the most. He declined their advice to stay with one or the other educated white women who had chased him. James was slow to notice women chasing him. He rarely chased them but he had chased Mary, much to her family's puzzlement. Erin accepted James first, even once said that he grew up similarly to how she grew up, in some ways.

What Erin lacked the insight to notice was storytelling, which bonded James and Mary. James had lived in many place, Mary only in the Cariboo; but each had a gift for telling engaging tales. Telling them to each other probably brought them together. Years together kept them together in spirit even across distances, and half a world separated them now.

"What are the Strait of Mocha again?"

"Strait of Malacca, Erin," Mary gently corrected, ever the mediator, as she was in her paid job of coordinating Williams Lake's social agencies, now expanding to include ones formerly under government control.

"The Strait of Malacca is a waterway that connects the Pacific and Indian Oceans. Lots of ships go through there. It's as important to Asian shipping as the Panama Canal is to American shipping. James went there to see how the Indonesians and Malaysians are taking it over, and regulating international shipping. Many shipping companies are bankrupt, of course, but shipping continues there, mostly run by worker-owned coops and national governments."

"Is it dangerous for James?" Erin asked.

"There was some danger when sailors and dockworkers and factory workers were seizing ships, but resistance by ship owners and paramilitaries melted away when they saw how outnumbered they were. James arrived after the danger subsided. He went because a friend in the Vancouver Commune got it to send James with an observer delegation. Vancouver sailors, dockers, and others connected to shipping are taking over, have pretty much taken over, that city's shipping. They want to learn from the Asians. A few Malaysians and Indonesians came to Vancouver, too."

"It's like an exchange, then?"

"Yep."

"When will James return?"

"In a few weeks, two months max."

"He's pretty brave to go across the world," Erin said. "I wouldn't do it."

"You'd be surprised what you would do, Erin," Mary replied. "Today you stared down the government social workers, criminal lawyers, and others who judged and jailed our people for generations. That was brave."

"It didn't feel brave then. They were so nervous about their future that it was as if I and the other band social development workers ran the meeting."

"You did run the meeting, Erin. Remember that old talk about 'The Red Road?' I recall that you used such talk in addictions counselling sessions, to clean up addicts by restoring their identity and traditions."

"I did indeed, Mary. It worked so well that I don't do it much anymore. Now I seem to have a new, bigger job."

"The Red Path."

"Huh?"

"Before James left, he coined the phrase 'The Red Path,' a title of the movement we're in. It includes The Red Road that you and I know about, and the socialism that James knows about. We indigenous people are taking over here, on our land. Other people are taking over the settler institutions and businesses on this land, and around the world, much of it on Indian land. The Red Path."

"Catchy title."

"So how'd it go today, Erin?" Mary asked.

"We got talking about oil, of all things. I didn't expect that. I thought we'd talk about us taking over our own social service and court systems, which we talked about. The government people and many lawyers have agreed to help, on our terms, on terms decided by people around here, not by people in Victoria or Ottawa."

"But then someone brought up transportation. You know that bands pay travel costs, governments pay travel costs, accommodation, and whatnot to people who go away to treatment or trial, to relatives who visit people in jail. I had no idea how much the oil companies make from this, or made from this, until a provincial government social worker started talking about it. It was Kathy Danshin. You met her a few months ago, briefly, at a conference here, just as the system was falling apart."

"I remember Kathy," Mary said. "She didn't seem as nervous as the others, even though it seemed they were all about to lose their jobs."

"She's older and she went through it before, in the early 2000s, when the provincial government laid off people and contracted out their work. I'm glad that got reversed. It was so much more expensive, and did a crappier job."

"Anyway, Kathy's seniority kept her in a job, near the top of the heap in the Cariboo. She has access to all kinds of government documents, including fuels costs, of all things. She said that we still need to travel for our work, even after we take it over from the government and the few contractors left in it. She told us about the local Transition Centre she visited."

"Aren't those the former gas stations?" Mary asked.

"Yes. Well, with the oil companies kaput, and refinery workers running the exploration, refining, and retailing of oil and gas, Transition Centres are the new gas stations; but they're more than gas stations. I didn't know how relevant they were to my field until Kathy mentioned them."

"They do more than sell gas, then?"

"They do indeed, little sister. According to Kathy, selling gas is only one part, and a shrinking part, of what Transition Centres do. Their main role is to guide the transition to a post-carbon society, a society that doesn't burn oil."

"That's a tall order, Erin," Mary said.

"Yes it is, and it's relevant to us social development folk. The local Transition Centre Committee, that runs all the gas stations in the Cariboo, including the native gas bars, has a social worker on it. That's because the committee understands that social workers need to travel, for court, for visitations, for all kinds of reasons."

"Is Kathy the social worker on the committee?"

"You bet she is. It also includes a representative from each indigenous nation: one Shuswap, one Carrier, one Chilcotin. There are also a maintenance person, a shipping person, an accountant, an engineer, an ecologist, and a couple other people."

"An ecologist on a committee running gas stations?"

"They are gas stations now, but they are transforming into post-carbon transportation centres. Hence the name Transition Centres. As the transition progresses, the ecologist will become more important, but the others will stay on. A post-carbon economy needs engineers, accountants, and shippers, too. The engineer is a petroleum engineer from Alberta. Kathy calls him "Our refugee from the tarsands.""

"The tarsands are closed, I recall reading," Mary said.

"Yes. The world never needed that oil at the price of such environmental destruction. Now it doesn't need it at all, since the military has shrunk so much."

Mary had a thoughtful look. Erin knew that a connection was coming. Her sister could connect the most disparate notions.

"Erin, what James is doing in the Strait of Malacca is connected to what Kathy is doing here. He's sort of up the line, at the shipping end. Lots of oil tankers go through that strait. They bring oil from Arabia to America."

Erin noticed that Mary used the new name for what had been several countries just a few years ago. Arabians and their many foreign workers had taken over the oil industry and deposed the tyrannical governments that had depended on it for their power. Tyrant loot cached in European and American banks had come back, due to public pressure in Arabia, Europe, and America. Now Arabian oil workers, including foreign ones, had decent livings in a democratic country.

Mary continued. "James is across the world seeing how others run the shipping of oil. Vancouver is retooling closed refineries to process that oil. Kathy is on a committee to help distribute it in the Cariboo."

"You sure can connect things, Mary," Erin marvelled.

"I had lots of practice when I coordinated the union of all the social agencies in the Cariboo. Others besides me are starting to see connections, now that they're no longer distracted by empty consumerist thrills."

Erin felt James coming on, via Mary.

"I won't turn into James and preach socialism at you, Erin. It's just that he and I seem to be on the same path, but we got there from different directions."

"The Red Path?" Erin asked.

"The Red Path," Mary replied.

Canada's biggest port, Vancouver, was welcoming more oil tankers than a few years ago. The cancellation of the Enbridge Northern Gateway Pipeline, the contraction rather than expansion of volume in the Kinder Morgan pipeline, meant that oil came to Vancouver more by water and less by pipeline than before. Almost no oil came by rail: rail spills, consequent blockades and the nationalization of Canada's rail system had taken "derailed oil" in a good way. Canada needed those trains and tracks to ship freight that had been wastefully shipped by truck for too many decades.

Enbridge. Kinder Morgan. No more. Worker-owned co-ops or government agencies now. Big trucking companies? Gone, worker-owned, or nationalized.

The tankers floating into Vancouver were double-hulled or better, and inspected before departure, en route, and upon arrival. Enforcement and fines were so rigorous that every sailor knew that safety, not some distant financial oligarch, guided him.

One reason that the Vancouver Commune sent a committee to the Strait of Malacca was to learn about Malaysian and Indonesian regulations. The Asian countries delegates came to Vancouver to learn about Canadian regulations. The funny finances behind shipping had been international for years; but now the environmental, and financial, regulation of shipping would be international, consistent, and demanding. "Flags of convenience" had been very inconvenient, even deadly, for the sea environment and for those who worked in it.

Now, a Somalian oil tanker, one of many seized even before the world's people seized the world's oil, would face inspection before it left Mogadishu, probably inspection by a Kenyan or Tanzanian agency along the way to Arabia, inspections docking, loading, and leaving, and possibly an inspection by a Diego Garcia agency on its way toward the Malacca Strait.

Diego Garcia is an island newly-wrested from military occupation by the United States. England had occupied it militarily first, and became the junior partner in the US empire. Now both countries had packed up their bombs and bombast and gone home. Diego Garcia's Indian Ocean location had given it strategic military importance. Now that same location gave it strategic environmental importance. People had cast the war machine off their backs. They and their environment now blossomed with potential.

The unholy alliance between the multinational military and the multinational oil companies had weakened with the sharp reduction of the military behemoth. For a time, oil companies tried to continue their international gangster ways, but without military backing more sizeable than a few private armies and their maniacal mercenaries, the oil companies had given up. Home country governments, including the United States, Netherlands, and Britain had refused to call out the dogs of war to recapture expropriated oil installations, foreign and domestic.

For generations, oil companies had been squawking in government ears, flapping around government circles, warning of shadowy foreigners who wanted to seize oil company assets. "They want to end our way of life," oil lobbyists had said; but governments finally saw that the "our" was only the oil companies, not the great masses of people, abroad and at home. The oil companies' lives were indeed over, but the home countries, the people in them, even the governments now felt the freedom of one who didn't know he was in a cage until the door opened and fresh air wafted in. The squawking oil companies had squawked their last. Like the dead parrot in the Monty Python sketch, the "Seven Sisters," the seven big multinational oil companies, had "ceased to be."

The oil was still there, and now it was for people, not for profit, for transition, not for the trickery of "green washing." Oil companies never intended a cleaner future for Earth. They intended to profit, by any means necessary: murder in the Niger Delta, deposing democratic government in Iran, co-opting government in Alberta, funding university research that suited their purposes and vilifying that which didn't, using the naked steel of the military, telling the naked lies of public relations. They had invested in alternative energy to green their pockets, not green the world. Their death grip on the throat of the world released, they would not grip the world with a pseudo-green hand now.

All those oil installations: wells, tankers, refinery and distribution networks, highly-skilled staff, seas of money, much of it finally seeing the light of day, the justice of public control. All that was now public property, the people's property.

Even the extant nationalized oil industries, such as in Norway and Saudi Arabia, felt the pinch of public pressure to behave or be gone. Wise heads on the North Sea and around the Persian Gulf decided to switch rather than fight.

These were practical people, eager to succeed against odds. They were happier when a hole produced oil than when it produced nothing, even if accelerated capital cost allowances made a dry hole as profitable to the company as a gusher. Now they would sink their expertise into the new and shifting ground of democratic control of the oil industry. There they would succeed against odds, not the odds of geology, but the odds of their own odd conditioning to slave for a wage, however big or small, and not for an ideal.

Idealists did not exactly gush forth from the dead oil companies, but there was enough of a trickle of them to keep the oil flowing. More importantly, among those idealists were many who would apply their considerable skills to the challenge of freeing society from its addiction to fossil fuels in general. Engineers and geologists here, like engineers in the auto industry, construction, and elsewhere, were recapturing the curiosity and drive that enticed them into these professions. Now they could indulge again, without looking over their shoulders for some financier who recently bought and sold these precious people.

———

Oil prices stayed high, despite the sudden drop in demand due to the dismantling of most of the world's military. These high prices were not to gouge the public, but to govern the transition to a post-oil world. Profits went to alternate energy development, much of the research already having been done, but not financially feasible to develop until governments dislodged the fossil fuel industry from its perch atop the tax system.

Full-cost accounting, that included social and environmental costs, now dominated the energy industry and doomed its fossil fuel segment. When one added humane wages and benefits, the remediation costs of polluted air, soil, and water, and the rising marginal cost of each newly-produced barrel of oil, million cubic feet of natural gas, or railcar of coal, oil, gas, and coal became much more expensive than solar, wind, and tidal.

These fossil fuels, legacies of millennia of organic matter would be used sparingly, mostly to convert sprawling utility and transport and distribution networks to local ones that would require less energy, or large systems that would run on renewable energy.

Technical people from the energy, transport, and utility industries were already gathering to coordinate a variety of conversion processes. Natural gas was flowing to auto plants throughout the world. As they did during World War Two, auto plants stopped making private automobiles; but now they made trains and buses, not tanks and jeeps.

The dismantling of the Alberta tarsands was freeing much specialty piping and a bewildering variety of metal and gauges and vehicles and many other tools, for use in the auto plants, now called transit plants, for use in tidal, wind, and solar generating stations, for use in rail and power and agricultural systems, for use in many ways in a sustainable economy. Mordor's tools became manna for transition. Most technical people had long known this could always be done. Now it was being done, with many transition challenges, and the bonus of many efficient techniques not discovered until people started working on the transition.

People are clever, and naturally good, given trust and the chance to shine. Human evolution set us above all species, but still firmly in nature, the final arbiter.

Was it too late? Had the Earth's atmosphere warmed until feedback loops kept Earth warming, even if fossil fuel combustion stopped completely? Recent summers had indeed been the hottest on record. Extreme storms had lashed Philippines, the US Gulf Coast, India, even Scotland. There were still extreme storms, extreme death tolls, and extreme destruction. Public responses had, however, been better lately: people had marched on governments and businesses and taken over the levers of response.

"Disaster capitalism" no longer existed, to profit from misery. Instead, local and regional and national governments, even national armies and navies, had conscripted wealth and equipment to reduce the misery born of natural disasters. Cuba was no longer the only, or even the main country that sent supplies and medical and technical people to disaster zones.

The United States sent a troop ship of supplies, doctors, engineers and trauma specialists, many of them Bengali-speaking, from Seattle to Bengal when a cyclone hit that country that had long exported its brightest to Europe and America. Upon their return, these USians had incubated communal republics along the west coast: Seattle, Portland, San Francisco, and Los Angeles among them. US President McKay's old political sparring partner Alex Foster was in the middle of this development.

McKay hoped that the communes of the West Coast would be friendly to the rest of the United States, in effect the former United States. Southern California and many southwest states were joining, rejoined Mexico. Vermont and Maine had joined Canada. She was confident that she would still be president after next week's election, and happy to give up some presidential power if the referendums passed, which her sources told her they would.

Her people were being more peaceful than she had expected them to be. Perhaps taming the shrill media and reducing inequality of income had helped bring people together. Those dictates from her recent speech probably irritated the powerful, but they could do nothing except agree. Millions of people supported her. Peaceful people. Hopeful people. She would do what she could for them, which included getting out of their way when they wanted to do what was good for one another, for the land, and for the future.

Of the people, by the people, for the people. At last. She wondered how Alex Foster was doing. Probably singing to school children about Joe Hill, or perhaps a new song about a Joe Hills, safe not shot, planning not reacting, organizing joyfully, without fear.

Interesting times indeed.

———

Farther west, across the Pacific Ocean, people were on the move. Many in the communes along North America's West Coast knew about this migration headed their way. Most agreed. People who were moving toward income equality could not reject people moving toward population equality. It was not so much imperialism's chickens coming home to roost, as the laboring masses which had enriched the Minority World coming to get their due.

    James Devlin saw some streams of ships from South Asia go through the Malacca Strait. In Indonesia with the Vancouver Commune shipping delegation, he expected tankers and cargo ships of inert fuel and freight, not ships, large and small, of human migrants. His Irish ancestors had migrated on "Coffin Ships," on which many Irish died before reaching America. These ships were better equipped, less crowded, but ubiquitous in the Strait. Their passengers were bound for the Americas, as his ancestors had been. History was repeating itself, but not a farcical imitation of a tragedy. This was a comedy, a drama with a happy ending.

    An Indonesian immigration activist had told James about the One to Five Movement, based in Africa and Asia, and sanctioned by the United Nations. It was voluntary transfer of population, from more to less dense areas. For example, teeming Nairobi, Kenya, in Eastern Africa, was sending shiploads of volunteers through the Red Sea to Libya, which had lower population density. Each country had a revolutionary socialist government, and they shared migration and settlement expenses. Densely-populated Gujarat, newly-independent of India, was sending shiploads of volunteers to New Zealand, which now boasted a coalition government of Maoris and settlers. Western Sahara, now independent of Morocco, accepted Nigerian migrants. India and Bengal were sending people to North America, whose governments shared the costs, as Kenya and Libya shared the costs of the Kenyan migrants.

    Some migrants were climate change refugees, from the advancing Sahara Desert, from Pacific Islands and coastal cities sinking under rising seas, and even new Dustbowl Refugees from US states such as Nevada and Oklahoma. No more Las Vegas. No more Caesar's Palace. No more Mafia. The stressed Oglala Aquifer had sighed, almost empty of water, and houses made on sand, the culture made of sand, had collapsed.

    Los Angeles and Vancouver were packed cities already, but the surrounding land, especially north of Vancouver and away from the Los Angeles desert, was not as crowded as the lands the Asians were leaving. The Vancouver Commune delegate to the upcoming Canadian constitutional conference had many propositions, financial and cultural, that would benefit Canada and its newest inhabitants.

"No one is illegal" has been the slogan of a movement to recognize migrant rights. Now it was becoming the law of many lands, including Canada and the United States. They still had wide open spaces, in Asian and European eyes. The United States and Mexico had dismantled the border fence, and re-deployed the border guards to help rather than to hinder migrants.

The "One to Five" in the "One to Five Movement" meant that a country had to take one migrant for every five people in its population. A person, any person in the world, could cross any border of any country of lower population density than her birth country. The welcoming country was obliged to support her. She had a year to become self-supporting, which was becoming easier as cooperatives replaced businesses, people services replaced profit services, and labor-intensive ecological and agricultural industry replaced oil- and chemical-driven industry. Canada, with 40 million people, was bound by United Nations rules to accept up to eight million migrants. James Devlin hoped his country was up to the cultural challenge.

Chapter 9: Canada, Reconstituted

"Albert! Albert Daniels? What are you doing in the Prince George train station, you old siwash renegade?" Kathy Danshin exclaimed.

"I'm the constitutional delegate for the Chilcotin, my Doukhobor darling," Albert replied. "You look pretty good for an old Russian. Too bad Doukhobors don't take their clothes off in public anymore."

"Albert, you haven't changed. Still got foot-in-mouth disease, I see. I'm the delegate for the Cariboo."

"You from one side of the Fraser River, me from the other side. Look out, Ottawa!" Albert said. "Seriously, I'm glad you're the one from the Cariboo. I could always talk to you. You always made sense. How's Roy?"

"He left me three years ago, Albert. More precisely, I left him. Always eager for adventure, he went north to work in the oil patch around Fort Nelson."

"Do you hear from him?"

"The last news I heard was sad: he got mangled on a drill platform and died a few days later in Grande Prairie hospital."

"I'm sorry to hear that, Kathy. He was sometimes full of himself, but we could talk. I won't say I know how it is when a close one dies, because it's different for everybody. When Paula died, people spoke the standard words of comfort to me, but it was I who found true comfort."

"That's so good, Albert. She was special. Nobody could fill her moccasins. Nobody should try," Kathy said pensively. "So here we go, two single people, battered and bruised by life, but on yet another adventure."

"It's a three-day train trip, Kathy," Albert said. "I'm sure we'll have plenty to talk about, old times, nowadays, the future. It's funny how life throws people together, eh?" His voice trailed off.

Fifteen minutes later, the train shuddered into motion, and east out of Prince George. The pair sat across from each other. Kathy faced forward, where the train was going. Albert faced backward, where the train was leaving. The settler looked ahead, the Chilcotin behind; but they shared seats, shared a train, and as the Rocky Mountains loomed ahead, they shared dreams of a bright future informed by the best traditions of the past. These two could talk to each other, and talk they would, across mountains, prairie, Canadian Shield, and along the Ottawa River valley.

This constitutional conference would be more democratic than the conspiracy of financiers, political lackeys, and literary hacks who conjured Canada in the 1860s. That was a speculative venture disguised as a nation. This would be a nation, ad mare usque ad mare, for people, not for profit. Albert Daniels and Kathy Danshin had ideas on how to make a better community, even a better country. More important, they were open to ideas from others, and the 47 others coming from across Canada, and the United Nations delegate, would have plenty of ideas.

"Good to be back behind the wheel, eh, Rosalee?" Holly said after hopping onto the running board.

"Damn right, babe," Rosalee replied. "It's like riding a bicycle. It comes right back to a woman. It's as if I never left the driver's seat."

Holly got in the passenger's seat.

"How are Walter and Leon doing, now that you're a happy reunited family?"

"Any better and it would be illegal, Holly. Walter has new energy in the mills and among the trucks and trailers. He's apprenticing a couple youngsters, one a woman. He seems to be having a second youth."

"Not a second women, I hope."

"Not a chance. This is a young white girl. Walter has chased white women before, but he's older and wiser now. He's a welder, and he only has a torch for me, girlfriend. He's happy to be back with me and Leon. Did you hear about Leon?"

"Nope. Good news, I hope."

"I hope so, too. He's only sixteen, seventeen by Christmas, and he's off to Vancouver for a four-month internship after Christmas."

"The school approved?"

"His physics teacher suggested the thing. Leon's going to work with the Vancouver Commune. They're turning lowlands into rice paddies, and building housing and resource centres for the immigrants coming from Bengal. Most won't settle in Vancouver, which is pretty crowded already; but they will bring useful skills the commune wants to tap. Vancouver is going for food self-sufficiency. It was lucky enough to get a handful of Cuban advisors. They're in great demand around the world. You know that Cuba has the world's greenest agriculture system, and that Havana feeds itself."

Holly had read about that in a new newspaper published in Williams Lake. The People's Tribune published in the same local plant that a distant press baron owned, until his company defaulted on its line of credit to Scotiabank, soon defaulted itself. Most of the staff stayed, and their skills now produced a very different newspaper from the corporate advertising rag whose decades-long masquerade as journalism had finally ended. People who had been shilling for the now-defunct Chamber of Commerce, popularly known as the Chamber of Nonsense during its absurd pre-death scrambling for public subsidy and sympathy, now wrote real news that mattered to ordinary people.

Many inches of the paper sported news written by people, unfiltered, frank, and inspirational. The Cuban agriculture story was a few issues back. Area ranchers and market gardeners were agitating for Vancouver to lend them a Cuban agronomist or two. One of the market gardeners described Havana's "Special Period" in the 1990s, after Soviet oil and chemicals stopped flowing and Cuba learned to farm without such short-term helpers that led to long-term dependency, and soil depletion.

The most ecological farming country now had a world that welcomed, pleaded for, direction from it. United States President McKay had ended the U.S. embargo on Cuba with the stroke of a pen, to almost no public objection, only a few old Cuban fascists and their brainwashed brethren in South Florida. Cubans were helping redesign US agriculture, and medicine.

Holly had read the article and shown it to Randy, who was expanding his vegetable garden, as were many people in Nemiah, and elsewhere in the Cariboo-Chilcotin. It's a dry land, but lush in places. The rhubarb planted in Barkerville in the 1860s by Chinese gold miners and traders still bloomed, for example. Barkerville was more mountainous than Nemiah. If Barkerville, why not Nemiah?

Barkerville and Nemiah. The two places embodied two sides of a contested history, a history long told in the one-dimensional tune of sturdy, quirky settler pioneers coming to an empty land, the indigenous people comic asides rather than original stewards of that land. More recently, indigenous writers and even some settler writers had been correcting this distortion. These visionaries unrolled, on paper, that settler tool, the symphony of indigenous cultures, the Cariboo's true history. Settler revisionist histories still had their place, as examples of how not to write history, as one-sided piffle rationalizing the displacement of indigenous people, as dark chapters in a dark phase of history. Piercing insights punctured that darkness with rays of truth.

History has phases. The moon has phases. Moonlight brings people together, Sarah told Holly when Holly brought the Cuba article to Randy. Sarah was a one-note tune, Holly thought at the time; but that tune was growing on Holly.

Randy, making pea fences of hockey stick shafts and chicken wire, looked quite at home in his garden. Interesting guy. Randy had been so happy to see Holly that he dropped his hammer on his foot as he climbed over a pile of hockey sticks to greet her. They made fences all afternoon, for that garden and several others in Nemiah.

Holly and Randy mended fences, too.

"Hello, hello, is Holly there?" Rosalee interrupted the reverie. "Are you coming with me or not? There's a truck waiting for you on West Fraser Road. Walter has fixed so many trucks and trailers and we're so short of drivers that everyone who can drive will drive. You ready?"

"Let's go, then. Tell me about Leon on the way to my truck, gear gal."

The truck rumbled north toward the West Fraser Road. The train rumbled east toward Ottawa. Organized, unified, motivated Chilcotins, the colonizers' worst nightmare come true. Indigenous people, long on the frontline of struggles against resource pillage, led the Cariboo-Chilcotin, most of Canada, and many places in the world. The eight generation was alert, and busy.

A new song was being written, metaphorically and literally. Felix Essex had taken his guitar from Stone to the Anaham meeting, listened, said little, and written a song, in 4:4 country time, A Major, of course, a good country key:

The Way is Now Clear

Chorus:
Talk the stories, talk to the young, listen to the old;
Our history is long and alive; we are not bought and sold.
Talk the stories, talk to the young, listen to the old:
The eight generation is here. The way is now clear.

Once a little girl got sick, and many caught it, too,
The settler's disease, smallpox, what could we do
But die in hoards, rest not in peace,
Survivors fearful as settlers increased.
The chief hanged, the land thieves spread
Like oil on our water, hiding our dead.
A few survivors knew the sad, sorry truth,
And told its tale, and our ways to the youth.

Chorus:
Talk the stories, talk to the young, listen to the old;
Our history is long and alive; we are not bought and sold.
Talk the stories, talk to the young, listen to the old:
The eight generation is here. The way is now clear.

Foreign laws, mission schools, exploiters came,
And made us ashamed of our Chilcotin name.
Stealing our trees, digging our ground, fouling our water,
They set father against son, mother against daughter.
Seven generations, bewildered, lost their way,
Selling their birthright for high or low pay.
Then a few stood up, stood against, risked all,
Not in casino thrall: a rise, not a fall.

Chorus:
Talk the stories, talk to the young, listen to the old;
Our history is long and alive; we are not bought and sold.
Talk the stories, talk to the young, listen to the old:
The eight generation is here. The way is now clear.

Old Sarah in her wheelchair, nothing to lose,
Was a spark lighting a long-dormant fuse,
"Get off my land," four words, four directions,
Healed the medicine wheel, made intersections
Among Indians and settlers long deceived
Now open to wisdom that elders conceived
As they told tales of days past and to come.
The people of the river will make the Earth one.

Chorus:
Talk the stories, talk to the young, listen to the old;

> Our history is long and alive; we are not bought and sold.
> Talk the stories, talk to the young, listen to the old:
> The eight generation is here. The way is now clear.

    I must remember to show this song to Erin Marseille, Felix thought. Her strong, happy voice can do it justice. It's a new song, but really based on an old song, finally come back to a people again brave enough to stand up for their past, present, and future.

    Felix Essex was on a creative roll, as were the Chilcotin people.

    As the train rolled east, it picked up constitutional delegates in the Prairies and Northern Ontario, some of the delegates indigenous. Albert and Kathy had new conversation partners, and the conversation expanded, sometimes in heat. The two delegates from Northwest and Northeast BC argued about pipelines with the delegate from Edmonton and the delegates from Northwest and Northeast Alberta. The Alberta delegates, all former oil company employees, agreed with the recent nationalization of pipelines, but they argued for more pipelines. The BC delegates, one a biologist, the other a former oil company employee, argued for a reduction in oil use and therefore in the need for pipelines. By Saskatoon, they had ironed out their differences.

    Then the soil scientist representing Northern Saskatchewan boarded the train, and the argument expanded to include oil spills, however few or many pipelines traversed Canada and the world. She had seen the Gulf of Alaska 20 years after the 1989 Exxon Valdez oil tanker spill. Oil was still on the beach, mere centimetres below the surface of the sand. "Soil Over Oil" was one slogan she was bringing to Ottawa, along with detailed arguments against biofuels, for local agriculture, chemical free, to maintain the soil on which that everyone's food supply depended.

    The oil people wisely ceded the debate, even after a mining engineer, the delegate from Northwestern Ontario, argued for more extraction in areas too marginal to farm, such as his rugged Canadian shield homeland. Albert was surprised to meet an indigenous person who was also a mining engineer. He told the miner about Simon van der Waals, implying that a mining engineer could repent of his ecologically-rapacious ways and work for the people. The engineer was interested, not only because he has lost his mining company had gone bust and laid him off, but also because he was applying his skills in various indigenous communities that his employer had been dividing, the better to despoil their land and water. As Albert got his contact information and gave him Simon's, Albert realized that a network he thought was a small oddity in the Chilcotin could reach across Canada, and perhaps beyond.

Kathy had moved among the passengers since the train left Edmonton. Now she was deep in conversation with the Métis child welfare worker who was Winnipeg's constitutional delegate. The Métis had long been on the indigenous child welfare forefront, in Winnipeg and Edmonton especially. Kathy was getting a real education on how an indigenous child welfare system worked, and getting a crash course in Métis philosophy. She hadn't known there was such a discipline as Métis philosophy. Back in the Cariboo, the Métis were few and operated in the shadows of the larger agencies run by settlers or status Indians.

It seemed to Kathy that here was a true Canadian, a person from this land, an inspiring combination of the best of the settlers and the best of the Indians. By Sudbury, Kathy knew more about the Battle of Seven Oaks, Louis Riel, Gabriel Dumont, and the 1869 Manitoba provisional government, whose authority the Hudson's Bay Company had recognized; she knew about the swindling away by speculators of Métis land scrip, she knew some Mischif, the Métis language amalgam of French and Cree; she knew the details of the Supreme Court of Canada decision that Métis had indigenous rights.

Kathy Danshin knew she had a friend in Ottawa, a place she had never been. Ottawa to her Doukhobor ancestors was a distant authority that outlawed Doukhobor customs and jailed people who dared to practice them. And here Ottawa had welcomed these refugees from oppression in Czarist Russia.

Then there was Albert, less full of himself than he had been in years past. He was so different from Kathy's ex-spouse, her "wasband." Good man, Albert. Good heart.

The train rolled into the Ottawa River Valley and stopped an Arnprior to pick up its last delegate, a anti-globalization movement veteran who had convinced Southwestern Ontario to send her to the constitutional conference in Ottawa. From London, she had been in Ottawa for a few days. Azza Nassar had bused to Arnprior to meet the many delegates coming from Western Canada.

Azza really liked National Bus, the public utility that had taken over Greyhound after it whined once too often for subsidy and to cut unprofitable routes. Most Greyhound drivers and station workers stayed on: they needed the jobs, and they found a freedom and attentive management, their own co-workers, who inspired them to work harder than they had ever worked for Greyhound. Routes were expanding, not contracting, and National was negotiating with auto and oil refinery workers, and even with the post office for new, more ecological rolling stock, fuel purchases, and mail and banking couriers for the post office and its network of banks.

Ottawa had given National a courier monopoly in Canada: Loomis, Purolator, UPS, and all the companies which had only served the rich and profitable areas were gone now. Some officers of Loomis's international arm, DHL, were in jail in various countries, for running shady operations, shipping arms, laundered money, and other shady stuff. Canadian Loomis officers had talked fast to stay out of jail themselves, most of them.

The post office, busy with its foray into banking, was happy to trade its mail shipping, and vehicles, to National, for National's financial and ticket operations. It was a big joint venture, working out many start-up bugs, but motoring along.

For many Central Canadians, Western Canada started in Thunder Bay, the Prairies and Western Cordillera being mere mysterious extensions. Azza Nassr knew better. She appreciated the size of the land that the people, finally, were about to govern.

What a bewildering variety of people she met on this train during its roll into Ottawa. She had a good feeling about them all, singly and as a group. Azza's feelings were usually accurate. They had saved her life more than once, during some pitched battles in London and elsewhere in Ontario, and the world. She seemed to know when to face, and when to run from danger.

"She who fights and runs away, lives to fight another day," she remembered from the Bob Marley song. Another day was here. Azza Nassar was glad she had lived to see it.

"I would like to welcome you all to the Canadian Constitutional Conference, CCC for short," Prime Minister Amy Knight said to the fifty delegates gathered in the Glebe Community Centre in South Ottawa. "We are here to make a new Canada, relevant to a new world."

Some cheers.

"Everything is negotiable this week, people. The British North America Act of 1867 served Canada for generations, the Constitution Act of 1982 patriated and updated that founding document, the Charter of Rights and Freedoms that same year recognized people long ill-served by earlier laws, for example indigenous people and women."

"Now is the time for a new constitution for a new Canada, a Canada governed from the bottom up, not from the top down."

Cheers.

"In this room are 49 people from this land, and one person from the United Nations, newly powerful in its world-leading role. Each of you 49 people represents a region of Canada. There are no delegates representing provincial governments or the federal government. It is within your power to abolish both levels of government. I have no say in the matter. The people of this land will decide, through your leadership. You are responsible to them, and they want a new society."

Louder cheers.

"Before I leave and you get down to the business of nation-building, I want to introduce Thenmozhi Chari, the United Nations delegate to this conference. Thenmozhi is from Tamil Nadu, one of the world's newest countries. Her first name means "honey-voiced," she told me when we met two days ago. She is only here as an observer and advisor. The U.N. sends one person to each constitutional conference to offer relevant international input to proceedings."

A greying but striking woman bowed to Knight and replaced her at the podium

"Good morning, delegates. I am Thenmozhi Chari from Tamil Nadu, here representing the United Nations. I don't know how honeyed my voice will be, but I am sure that you all will have sweet things to say in what is become a sweet world in which to live."

Cheers.

"Your government is your business, but your government influences the world, I hope in a positive way. I am here as an observer and advisor to help ensure that positive influence. I have one vote, the same as each of you has. You represent 49 regions that comprise Canada. Consider me your own delegate to the world."

"I know something about this land, which you can choose to call Canada at the end, choose to make part of another country, choose to make into more than one country. For now, let us call it Canada. I hope you will educate me further."

"This is not my first time here. I studied crop science at the University of Saskatchewan, and taught various courses and supervised various theses at the Universities of Alberta, Guelph, and Sherbrooke. I speak Tamil, Hindi, English, and French. My languages and my Canadian experience were the main reasons the United Nations sent me to this constitutional conference."

"I looked at the delegate list and I was happy to see some scientists on it. Science has many things, and a useful ethic to offer the world. Alas, science has in the past offered the world ways to kill its flora and fauna, including humanity. Now science can offer its ethic of critical thinking to a world more open to it now than at any time in human history, including the Enlightenment of the 17th and 18th centuries. It's also nice to have a couple lawyers in this room, to help codify what you all produce."

"She's very enlightening herself," Albert whispered wryly to Kathy. "Now I want to join the United Nations. Her crop science sorta grows on me. Fields to plow, heh heh."

Kathy stomped her runner on his foot under the table.

"Just kidding, Kathy. I'm listening, and I'm behaving myself." She cares, Albert thought. Good woman. Practical. People know where she stands. I know where she stands, including on my foot to keep it out of my mouth.

"As you work this week to devise a progressive way to govern this rich country, I will mingle among delegates," Chari said. "On behalf of the United Nations, I would like to thank you all for inviting me, and thank Canada for participating in the One-to-Five Movement. The Bengalis you are welcoming to your shores will be diligent additions to this great land. In fact, after this conference, I will visit, by invitation, the Vancouver Commune. It has asked me for advice on how to grow rice. I am glad that I am still a scientist and teacher, as well as a politician."

"A new politics requires a new cohort of worker politicians, people who know how to make things, do things, teach things, and most importantly, people willing to work together for a better world. I am confident that you are such people. Thank you for listening to me. I hope my words were as honeyed as those of your prime minister."

Loud cheers. Some thumping of tables.

Chari and Knight walked down from the stage, Chari to meet various delegates, Knight to her office. Each woman had a spring, almost a bounce, in her step.

Albert Daniels and Kathy Danshin watched the two women leave the stage. Both delegates were a little nervous, but they would depend on each other for support and direction during this historic week. They both had come a long way, from different cultural directions, but they were on one road, together, now.

The Red Road.

"Welcome, Holly," Walter said, opening the door. "I see that Rosalee didn't kill you in her truck."

"She's a good driver, Walter, and she's so happy to be back behind the wheel," Holly said. "She's also happy that she, you, and Leon are together again."

"Don't I know it, Holly. I'm a very lucky man."

"Remember that, Walter. Rosalee's right behind me. She's getting a few things out of my pickup, which we drove back in after we dropped off our big trucks. Where's the young architect?"

"He's talking to people in the building trades union hall, getting ideas before he goes to Vancouver after Christmas. Rosalee told you about that, eh?"

"Indeed she did. What a chance for the young squirt. I'm sure the builders have useful advice for him. It's nice that they're back in business, after all those years of non-union construction companies undermining them, setting them against one another."

"Sure is, Holly. I got back a bit early today and I made supper. Hungry?"

"Does a moose grunt in the fall time?" Holly replied.

"We have room for you, if you want to stay the night, too."

"Thanks, Walter. It sure is good to see you like this."

"I feel great, Holly, like a man reprieved from the gallows. Rosalee's the only one for me."

"You talking about me behind my back, Walter?" Rosalee said as she came through the door. "Good things, I hope."

"Nothing but," Holly said. "He even made supper for us road warriors."

"Well, I'm as hungry as a bear in the spring. Let's eat, and watch today's big news."

"Ready when you are," Walter said, going to the kitchen to plug in the kettle for tea.

"How is it around here, Rosalee?" Holly asked quietly.

"It's pretty good, Holly, almost like the old days, and getting better every day. We belong together."

"You did since you were ten years old, chasing rabbits in Nemiah. I'm glad it's working out."

"What about you and Randy? You chased rabbits together when you were ten, too."

"We'll see," Holly said. "We'll see."

They walked across the living room. Rosalee turned on the tv."

"Come and get it," Walter said from the kitchen.

Moose stew loaded into bowls, bannock in hand, they returned to the living room. Walter fetched the tea and cups.

Holly, chewing, said, "This is pretty good bannock, Walter."

"Just like mom used to make," Walter said.

Walter's late mother was legendary for bannock.

"Well, you're not there yet," Holly quipped. "Keep practicing. I'll eat your work and gauge your progress. I'm your official bannock tester. Dirty job, but someone's gotta do it."

"Yeah, you really seem to be suffering as you gauge that first piece of bannock, Holly. I think my bannock tester should bring her own jam, and a bag of flour once in awhile. We'll have a joint venture."

"Here comes the special report about the constitutional conference," Rosalee interrupted. "Look for Albert. I hear that he got to speak to the whole crowd."

The Canadian Broadcasting Corporation, now enjoying stabler public funding and collective self-management, began its newscast with the new music and a montage. A catchy, folksy ballad tune back dropped a montage of natural and man-made scenery that included an indigenous elder woman storytelling in a circle of children, a black nurse prescribing to a young man, a music teacher conducting teenage singers, and gardeners transplanting seedlings. As the last chord faded, the sun rose behind the busy Hamilton steelworks.

"Good evening, Canada and the world," an even, blue-eyed woman's voice intoned. "This is Gail Larsson with a CBC news special, about the Canadian Constitutional Conference, now finished its second of five days. Today, the 49 delegates from Canada's regions, and the one delegate from the United Nations, made great progress on many fronts. We now go to our reporter in Ottawa, Edward River, for details."

A young indigenous man with a pony tail came on the screen. He held a microphone. Behind him, delegates milled about, some looking at the camera."

"Thank you, Gail. Today the delegates built on yesterday's remarkable progress. You recall that yesterday they voted provincial governments out of existence, as expected. There was less resistance to that from Quebec and Alberta than had been anticipated. Sections 91 and 92 of the Canada Act, the updated British North America Act, are gone. In their place is a division of powers between the federal government and the 49 regional governments. Today saw the hammering out of that division, with a few loose ends to tie up tomorrow."

The screen split to River and the anchor woman, who asked, "Tell us the highlights of today's events, Edward."

"Well, Gail, today the regions agreed to make education, medicine, transportation, environmental protection, and banking federal government domains. This in effect expands federal powers, especially in the areas of education and medicine. There will be national standards for school and university funding, school curriculum, and doctor, nurse, teacher and paraprofessional training. The regions will administer, as they will administer almost every program; but the federal government will fund and monitor them."

"This must be something of a surprise to nervous federal politicians, Edward. They aren't part of this conference, and some worried that the conference would abolish federal as well as the provincial government."

"There was that concern, Gail. The conference had the power to abolish the federal government, but it didn't take much discussion to realize that Canada needs coordination among its regions. That brings up another big development today: elections."

"How will elections work, Edward?"

"Delegates voted for a proportional representation system. Each region will elect three members to the national parliament, by proportional voting. The party with the highest percentage of the vote gets the most representatives. If that party gets 75% of the vote, then it gets all three representatives for that region. If it gets 50-75%, then it gets two members. Any party with more than 25% gets one member for that region, to sit in the federal parliament."

"That's the new House of Commons," Gail said. "What about the senate?"

"It's gone, voted out of existence today, after a short debate that was more like a sigh of relief from the delegates than a debate."

"Edward, it sounds as if the conference made great progress today. Thank you. What's will tomorrow likely bring?"

"Gail, today seemed to be the most significant day of the conference, with the division of powers and the agreement on the new electoral system. Tomorrow will deal mostly with topics that flow from today's events: funding formulas, training and regulation of medical and educational people, and setting election dates and rules, for example. One new topic tomorrow will be the legal system. There are a few lawyers among the delegates, and they will articulate general legal principles, some of them familiar and in practice now, some new, for the new conditions rapidly coming about in our society."

"Well, keep us informed, Edward."

"Thank you, megwich, Gail."

"That was Edward River reporting from Ottawa, at the Canadian Constitutional Conference. We'll have analysis of the conference after this brief break."

A public service commercial came on the screen. It showed children in a playground. A voice over explained proposed changes to the public education system, including the friendly takeover of private schools, the abolition of educational fees, and the election of regional and national boards to revamp curriculum and reduce transportation distances for elementary school students. "Public education. It's for all our children, for all our futures," the voice concluded at the end of the minute.

"Did you see Albert behind that nenqayni reporter?" Walter asked.

"He was grinning like an idiot," Rosalee said. "I hope he looked more intelligent in his speech. I heard he made a short speech."

"I heard it was a good speech. He talked about Sarah and the roadblock, and also about the land in general, and child welfare," Holly said. "I watched it online at the shop after I drove my load in today. I was a little ahead of Rosalee, but she had a longer route and fuller load."

"How was your trailer, Holly? I think it's the one that I had the apprentices practice on the other day."

"You must be a good teacher, Walter. The trailer was just fine. Not a squeak, not a groan. How are the apprentices working out?"

"They're great. They're listening to this old man, and learning. It seems my brain still works."

Rosalee perked up. "You're not so old, Walter. Your brain isn't the only part of you that still works."

"Should I go into the other room, lovebirds?" Holly wisecracked.

"Stay for the news. See what the commentators make of today's events at the conference," Rosalee said. "We'll remember that this is family hour."

"OK. I'm here for a televised performance only, you two."

The news anchor came back on. "Welcome back, viewers. We have with us tonight Azza Nassar, the constitutional delegate from Southwestern Ontario, and Archie Ittaq, the delegate from Nunavut. Thanks for joining us after your busy day, delegates."

"It's a pleasure to be here," Ittaq said from across the table.

"Thank you for inviting us," Nassar said, from her seat between the anchor and the Inuk.

"First to you, Azza," anchor Larsson began. "What is the significance of today's conference results?"

"Gail," Nassar began, "today we made a new Canada, in effect. It's a Canada of democratic centralism. That means that it has a strong central government, informed by democratic representatives from its 49 regions. I think it was a good day, a historic day."

The anchor turned to Ittaq. "Archie, you came from a long distance, Nunavut. Did events turn out the way you hoped, for your region?"

"Yes they did, Gail; but it was close for awhile there, with the debate before the vote to abolish provincial governments. The debate wasn't long and it seemed to reach a consensus at the end, but one Quebec delegate and a couple Alberta delegates were nervous about cultural and property rights in a country without provincial governments."

"Yes, property was never an absolute right in Canada, but now it is even less so," Gail said. "And French speakers long had Quebec as their cultural champion."

"As Nunavut is for Inuktitut speakers, Gail," Archie said. "By the end of the debate, which was more like a discussion, the Quebec and Alberta delegates were satisfied that culture and property would be safe in the new country."

"If I may interject," Azza said. "By the time of the vote, the Alberta delegates seemed happier with the new economic than they had been with the old economic system. One told me that predictability is good in business and in government. She said that it didn't matter much to her region if that business was public or private, only that it efficiently served them."

"That sounds like a very interesting discussion you had," Gail noted.

"It was. I never expected to find so much common ground with someone from a background so unlike my own."

"Your background is legendary in this country, Azza," Paul observed. "We know about you up in Nunavut. I'm glad you're at the conference."

Azza Nassar seemed choked up, at a loss for words, unusual for one who had commanded legions of demonstrators with her eloquence through megaphones.

"Thanks, Paul. You have no idea how nice your words sound to me."

Holly said, "She'd be an interesting woman to meet, eh?"

"I wonder if Albert talked to her," Rosalee said.

"No stopping Albert," Walter said. "He could talk a dog off a meat wagon. I'd like to meet that Inuit guy. He looks like he knows the land. Did you notice his hands? They're strong, the hands of someone who has hunted, someone who has lived off the land."

"Well, now we have our land back. He probably has his land back," Rosalee said. "Speaking of land, Holly, are you going back to Nemiah tomorrow?"

"Yes I am. That mining engineer, Simon, wants me at some meeting about heavy equipment."

"How's he doing out there?" Walter asked.

"He's like one of us now," Holly replied. "The guy listens to the elders. He offers relevant suggestions in all sorts of areas: housing, power generation, even education."

"Education?" Rosalee asked, nervously.

"It's not as if he wants to plunk the mission school on us again," Holly explained. "He talks about training band members for all sorts of industrial jobs. His wife and their daughter moved into the bed and breakfast the other day. She's some kind of expert with traumatized children. She's really useful around the school, and with the hard teenagers. Her daughter grew up in Vancouver but she seems to jive with the local young adults. She's helping Randy with the gardens."

"How's Randy?" Walter asked innocently.

"He's fine," Holly replied. "I've been over to see him and Sarah a couple times. I'll probably go there this week. Her bannock is better than yours, Walter."

"Her grandson isn't too bad either," Walter replied, matching wits.

"Whatever!" Holly said, flashing her eyes at Walter. "Remind me to run over you the next time I have the chance, smart aleck."

"I'll jump out of the way, into Rosalee's waiting arms."

The special newscast over, a commercial came on, about the growing communal farm movement in the Niagara Peninsula, Saskatchewan and the Fraser Valley. Women walked in an apple orchard, baskets under their arms. A leathery-faced farmer looked at the prairie horizon. Children laughed at their blueberry-stained fingers as the Coastal Mountains loomed behind them, and farm workers loaded flats of blueberries into a rail car. "Land for the people. Food for the world," the voice over concluded.

"Well, this people better get to bed," Walter said. "Holly, you can have the hide-a-bed. The sheets and blankets are in the corner there. Leon will be back late. When he gets talking numbers and equations with people who know that stuff, Chris loses track of the time."

Rosalee and Holly exchanged a glance. Walter was so proud of his son, and so grateful to be back in Leon's life.

Chapter 10: Food, Clothing, and Shelter

"Happy New Year! Get up, lazybones!" Rosalee said to Leon. "You have two hours to get your calculators and computers and toothbrush and whatnot before Johanna and Maria come for you."

"Rrrrmph!" Leon Iqallie grunted, half asleep. "What time is it?"

"It's six in the big A.M., son of mine, and you're going to Vancouver, by invitation. Your internship starts on Thursday, but you're going today because Holly found you a ride."

"Thank her for me, Mom," Chris said, half awake. "It'll be nice to get there a few days early, to scope things out. Who am I going with, again?"

"Johanna and Maria van der Waals, the spouse and daughter of Simon. You remember Simon?"

"Yeah. He's pretty interesting, full of interesting ideas, surprising for an old guy. What are his spouse and daughter like?"

"You'll have all the way to Vancouver to find that out, young man. Get up and get organized. Your dad made breakfast. Holly's coming for us at 7. We gotta go out in the bush to help Dad and an apprentice fix a truck and drive it back. Someone broke down last night."

"Is is that white girl apprentice? I met her. She's interesting, too."

"I'm sure she is. You stay interested in Vancouver and your education, my young friend. Turning 17 last week doesn't free you from my wise guidance."

"Yes, Mom." Leon rolled out of bed and rubbed his face as he ambled to the bathroom.

Rosalee went to the kitchen. "Well, Spark, how you doin' after a sober New Year's Eve?" She walked up behind him as he worked at the stove.

"Best New Year's Day in years, Gears," he turned around quickly and hugged her. "People can have fun without booze on New Year's Eve, eh?"

Leon walked in. "Jeez, you two. You make me lose my appetite." His parents parted and breakfast appeared.

A half hour later, Leon was alone, packed, and waiting for Johanna and Maria. A half hour after that, the winter sky still orange from the sunrise, the three rolled through 150 Mile House on their way to Vancouver. Maria was behind the wheel, Chris was in the passenger seat, and Johanna was in the back, a pile of papers beside her, a laptop on her lap. Johanna and Maria had done most of the talking, and Maria most of that. Maria wasn't like the airheaded girls in his high school, Leon thought, primping their bodies instead of priming their brains.

"How you like Nemiah?" he asked.

"I really like it," Maria replied. "My blond hair and blue eyes really make me stick out there, but people talk to me when they see me puttering around with Randy. He's glad to have someone with gardening experience. Our Vancouver garden was the talk of the neighborhood. I'm learning a lot, from him and from his granny."

"They're an interesting pair, all right," Leon said. "You in school back in Vancouver?"

"I graduated last year. Mom and I are going down for a month to sort out the house and stuff."

"We're selling our house in Vancouver, Chris," Johanna said from the back seat. "Nemiah offered to build us one, sort of a model of sustainable housing. Simon's working on the plans. It's nice to have the bed-and-breakfast to live in until we finish the house, probably by June 1."

"I'd like to see those plans and that house," Chris said. "I'm going to Vancouver to work on housing, among other things. It's an internship my physics teacher helped set up. She'll give me course credit. It's like a term-long project. I'll report regularly to her."

"It's a marvelous opportunity," Johanna said. "Maria has something similar in mind. An apprenticeship, but in an area quite different from yours."

"I'm just thinking about it, Mom. Nothing's settled yet."

"What's it about?" Chris asked.

"Agriculture, believe it or not," Maria answered. "While Mom wraps up the house stuff, and her charity stuff, I might work with the Bengalis on the rice project."

"Really?" Chris said. "I'll be there some, too. This internship is about housing, but also about installing weirs, drainage systems, and buildings for the rice project, and for the people working in it. I'll also be out of town some, in the Fraser Valley, reclaiming farmland from the urban sprawl that now occupies it."

"We might run into each other at work," Maria said, now more enthusiastic for the apprenticeship that had once seemed more her parents' plan for her than her own plan.

"Well, you'll see each other regularly anyway, because you're staying with us in our Richmond house, Chris," Johanna said. "Lots of those Richmond 'monster houses' are becoming co-ops, some by the owners themselves, some by sale. I've always felt that our big house was too much for the three of us."

"I thought I was staying with Dad's cousin."

"That is, I hope you'll stay with us, Chris. I have a proposition for you," Johanna began.

I have a proposition for your daughter, Chris thought to himself.

"Our house needs some tinkering to get it ready for the new owners, some cooperative or other," Johanna said. "Simon assures me that you can do it. Nothing heavy. A few plumbing things and general yard work, mostly. We'll feed and shelter you for free if you stay with us. I'll be sure that the work doesn't interfere with your apprenticeship. Simon thinks it can enhance it, actually."

"I'd have to call my dad's cousin," Chris replied. "I don't think he'd mind. They're pretty crowded over by Guildford Mall. Richmond would be much closer to work for me."

"Use my cell phone when we get in range to call your dad's cousin," Johanna said. "We want to help, not start a family feud."

"It'll be all right, I'm sure," Chris said.

"I hope so," Maria said, every word of the conversation imprinted on her busy brain, like sprouting herbs in her Vancouver garden, or potatoes in the Snow Mountains of Nemiah. Nice place, Nemiah. Nice people. Nice guy, this handsome Chilcotin with the soft words and soft eyes.

In the back seat, Johanna smiled a bit and dug into her paper mountain for something charity or real estate sheet or other, happy that her only child had met someone motivated, and motivating.

Long drive to Vancouver. Lots to talk about. Lots to think about.

———

"The constitutional conference set clear and simple tax rules, Jennifer. Did you hear?" Mike Vidic said a couple days later, as they trolled financial records in Quesnel banks, having finished with the Williams Lake banks. The two cities' credit unions were merging, and financial officers in both cities wanted things consistent. Indian bands wanted a window into the proceedings. Mike Vidic was that window for the Chilcotin and Carrier and Shuswap bands. His Nemiah and Williams Lake work was making him much in demand, and much trusted by Indians, slow to trust, but solid when they do trust.

"Yes, I heard. It's a big improvement over that door stop called the Tax Act. I only know the highlights, from an email I got from a Six Nations friend in Montreal. I like the progressive, simplified tax brackets, and the few deductions."

The constitution conference had finished its work the day before, Friday. Jennifer Brant and Mike Vidic were on a day trip to Quesnel, mostly to meet their financial counterparts there, a prelude to coordinating a regional credit union system that covered both the Cariboo and Chilcotin regions.

Mike would also visit the Carrier tribal council offices, newly expanded due to their takeover of local government and not-for-profit child welfare functions, and some justice functions. Settlers long ran indigenous welfare and justice, badly for indigenous people.

Now indigenous people would run settler welfare, and listen to settlers more than settlers had listened to indigenous people. No "60s Scoop" of children, a genocidal attempt to remove a child from her culture and implant a new culture in her, Franken-social work. Sentencing circles and restitution would replace jails and revenge, never more than a myopic insult to the dignity of the jailed and the jailer.

Taxes would have a fierce and progressive simplicity. Income taxes, first concocted during World War One as a temporary measure, were to be temporary by constitutional fiat: ten years and gone. But until they went, they would greatly equalize wealth and income in Canada, and increase government revenues.

Annual income up to $60 000 would be tax-exempt. Income between $60 000 and $150 000 would pay a 50% tax on every dollar above $60 000. Income between $150 000 and $500 000 would pay a 75% tax on every dollar above $150 000. Income above $500 000 would pay a 90% tax on income above that level. Inheritance taxes were the same rates. This was more progressive than taxes had been in decades, but between the end of World War Two and the early-1960s, there had been a 90% marginal tax rate on the highest-income people. They had still lived lavishly enough, and Canada had built a decent society with the revenue.

The era of tax cuts for the idle rich, who invested in their luxuries rather than in Canada's people and future, were over. More equality benefits the rich as well as the poor, and produces a healthier population, as Scandinavian countries had proved for decades. England and America had ignored that, eviscerated their tax systems on the advice of the rich, and had suffered a decline in their infrastructure and their people's health. The main tax cut would be 20% per person who participated in the One-to-Five Movement by housing a foreign migrant. This rate would rise or fall depending on how well Canada approached its target of eight million immigrants by the ten-year deadline.

Marcel Dubrovsky's sturdy crew of number crunchers, working under Prime Minister Knight, had been the main designers of this system. The constitutional conference had invited them on its last day of proceedings. The three accountants and two lawyers who were delegates recommended it, and the body agreed to it.

Dubrovsky's team had anticipated this invitation. They came with the general outline of the tax system. Discussion among the delegates decided the final numbers, and the ten-year lifespan of the system. Dubrovsky was proudest of that limited lifespan: income tax implies wage work, and wage work is exploitative by nature. End wage work, and end the need for tax. He doubted that he would see that stage, but he was certain that younger people around him would work to bring it about.

The two financial wizards, Jennifer Brant the Six Nations Indian and Mike Vidic the Slavic immigrant, talked about the new tax system together, and with the Quesnel credit union people. Vidic summarized it for the tribal council, happiest that the constitutional conference had abolished the Indian Act. Their council was a creature of that abomination that had informed South Africa's apartheid system, Mike knew from listening to the van der Waals, however; but the tribal council had decades of practice in many areas, and the trust of the settler population to expand its services to touch their lives in positive ways.

"Facts on the ground," as Zionists had said during their ethnic cleansing of Palestine from 1947 until the recent dissolution of the Jewish state and creation of a single, secular Palestine. The tribal council in Quesnel, like tribal councils all over Canada, had "facts on the ground," but positive, inclusive facts. Their traditional belief, that people steward the land rather than own it, would infuse their practice. Now they planned to share the land, the original intention of their ancestors, from whom settlers had swindled the land.

Circumstances had swept away many retrograde notions, such as private property, private land. Most people adjusted, but some needed more of the education that circumstances bring to alter their consciousness.

"Life is not determined by consciousness, but consciousness by life" was emblazoned above the local tribal council's main lobby desk. Vidic remembered the phrase from his mother's instruction: it was from The German Ideology, by Karl Marx and Friedrich Engels. He wondered how these Indians a world away in time and place from the 19th century conditions in which Marx and Engels wrote, not to mention around the world from his mother's beloved Yugoslavia, found this phrase to decorate their headquarters.

There had been old communists in the Quesnel wilderness for decades. Perhaps one of them came out of the woodwork with the axiom. Who knows?

Many old-timers were afoot with new energy, all over the world, including Indonesia.   James Devlin was almost at the end of his time there for the Vancouver Commune, but only beginning to see the significance of the education that some old Indonesians had given him.

A few had survived the 1965 coup d'état that deposed the democratic government and murdered a sea of communists. Until that slaughter, Indonesia had the world's largest communist party outside China and the Soviet Union. Muslim leftists there made the imperial powers as nervous as Muslim leftists in Iran had done in the early-1950s. Each country entered a dark era of anti-communism, anti-progress, anti-democracy, fueled by Muslims convinced that the left, including the Islamic left, was their religion's and their countries' enemy.

The German Nazis had slaughtered Ernst Roehm and his leftist threat in 1934. The United States spies had undermined Iranian President Mossadegh's socialist government in 1953. The western-educated Mossadegh only wanted Iran to have the social and economic privileges that England enjoyed. "Socialism is fine for Britain, but not for Iran," was one English leaders' quip, before the US military stole back the Anglo-American Oil Company from the Iranians, whose oil wealth buttressed the British Empire for decades.

In 1965, the United States, having inherited the British mantle of mangling the world for money, overthrew Indonesia's government. The bloodbath that ensued spared few, but some. A few of them, and their newly-emboldened protégés, educated James Devlin in Indonesian history, which had similarities to the history of his ancestors' country, Ireland.

James was on a ship full of Bengali migrants bound for Canada, getting another education, and educating his fellow passengers, about to become Canada's newest citizens. And they would be citizens, not temporary foreign workers, not part of that discredited, defunct scheme to depress Canadian wages and offer foreigners none of the rights that previous immigrants had enjoyed upon reaching Canada.

James was glad that the Canadian Constitutional Conference had decided to keep a federal government. Until something better came along, and that seemed possible, the nation state was a useful tool for the world's people. Regions had gained immigration/emigration authority; but the immigration documents, formalities now, not terrors as in the past, would welcome these Bengalis to Canada. They would be free to live anywhere in Canada, but already they were organizing themselves to be useful to their new country: most would stay in the West, and lend their agricultural and cultural expertise to Vancouver, Calgary, and other communal cities trying for food sovereignty and self-sufficiency.

Mass demonstrations in Vancouver had seized the port and blockaded the bridges. The city police had joined the movement, and the Chilliwack military base had lacked the interest and probably the ability to overturn it. Mass demonstrations in Calgary following oil company bankruptcies and the city government's own bankruptcy had incubated the Calgary Commune. Now, people from across the city, full of solidarity for these Canadian people's movements, were coming to help build the new society, the shell of the old society falling away like a caterpillar's cocoon.

What an educated bunch, what an enthusiastic bunch, James thought, each time he sat in on the Bengalis discussions. There were agronomists, an architect, textile experts and workers, even some university social science and literature professors. Lucky Canada, getting a shipload of such special people!

One Bengali was a seed expert, from the Vandana Shiva Brigade that had wrested control of the land of India, Nepal, and Bengal from Cargill, Monsanto, and other now-extinct multinational agribusiness firms. They were better known as "agrideath" firms for the farmer suicides their rapacious practices had caused. The late Indian physicist Vandana Shiva had left physics for food activism, specifically the saving of heritage seeds and consciousness-raising about the toll of human misery born of corporate control of agriculture, of corporate control of land.

Food, clothing, and shelter, human needs; but joy was also a human need, and joy was in great supply across Canada lately, and elsewhere in the Americas and the world. Vancouver would grow rice, and have community gardens everywhere possible. The Cuban advisors would help see that begin, and leave the people well able to finish the job. The Fraser Valley grows more densely-populated as people dismantled the pavement and sprawl that sat on that excellent farmland.

Across the country, Montreal's and Toronto's derelict textile mills would hum again, thanks to Asians who had formerly worked at home for slave wages, now leading a re-localization of clothing production. By the time the Bengali boat docked, many regions applied to play host to the migrants. There were twice as many applications as passengers.

Luckily there would be more boats, more special people come to Canada. Indeed, Canada would send some people overseas, some to learn, as James Devlin had learned, some to settle, in a world now one, not bled into conflict by the arbitrary lines called borders, scratched onto maps, scratched into lives.

Some of the migrants knew about housing in floodplains, having survived many floods in their native Bengal, especially its eastern part, former Bangladesh. Millions lived mere metres, or less, above sea level. The Dutch aren't the only people who know how to corral the sea. Netherlands welcomed migrants from Bengal, and from its former colonial possessions in the Western Pacific: Indonesia, Timor Leste, Papua New Guinea, and Aceh, new countries, out from under the uncomfortable umbrella of Indonesia.

What's not possible? James Devlin thought, as he cheerily bedded down below decks and the ship chugged across the Pacific, toward Canada. He was returning to a very different country from the one he had left only a few weeks before.

In Richmond, Leon Iqallie and Maria van der Waals walked along the beach, much of it covered in construction materials for the rice works. Some beach would remain open for walkers and dreamers. No beach would be private

The sun was setting in the west, an optical illusion as old as the consciousness of this clever species that finally figured out the Earth's rotation, not the Sun's movement, caused the sunset. Refraction streaked orange and pink over the

Georgia Strait. The two young people had done several days of hard but satisfying work.

"There are fewer pets than I remember," Maria observed. A few people walked dogs big and small, but as the sense of community grew, people devoted themselves to one another, and did not need the blind obedience and comfort that pets had long provided the marginal, neurotic, selfish, and autocratic. Blind obedience was over. Eyes were open around the world.

Chapter 11: The Land

Ian Helting barked at Max Levins, "Corporal, this outfit will be on the train to Thunder Bay at noon. Can you manage it?"

"Yes, sir," the bespectacled batman said, a sea of small and large details flowing in his mind.

The largest detail was the Canadian military's new role in Canada and the world. No longer was it the lapdog of this or that empire. Now its awesome but shrinking power would repair the land and lives it had harmed in foreign lands, and do some heavy social lifting in Canada.

Helting's Wainwright army, fresh from its "visit" to Cold Lake to ensure that air base's loyalty, was going to Haiti. Haiti, the site of the world's first successful slave revolt, in 1805, was finally free from foreign domination and domestic tyranny. Imperial France had retaken its former colony soon after the revolt, bled it white with unfair demands for reparations, and for generations dominated this rich, beautiful land. The United States, inheritor of empires, wayward colonial spawn of the British Empire, had dominated Haiti after the French Empire collapsed with the end of World War Two.

Still, the liberation struggle continued, in the early-2000s electing Jean-Bertrand Aristide, a former priest and fervent anti-colonialist. Canada's participation in the 2004 coup that overthrew him, and Canada's subsequent training of Haitian police and military in suppression, meant that Canada had much to atone for, now that Haiti was free again, forever. Ian Helting knew and liked his mission: rebuilding roads and buildings, disarming paramilitaries, overseeing the RCMP's de-programming of the police that it had trained in torture and other tyrants' techniques.

Helting was glad this was the swan song of the RCMP, and that it would return to Canada, and dissolution, after this mission. Rogue RCMP across the prairies had caused his troops no end of irritation, but they had been minor irritants standing in the way of the progress, nostalgic fascists from an anti-democratic police force that had outlived by 1920 whatever usefulness it might have had, and Helting knew enough history to doubt that this colonial concoction had ever been useful. It's increasing aloofness from public scrutiny had helped damn it in public and governmental eyes.

What was left of the RCMP would go to Haiti under Helton's army command. It would behave, do what it was told, and serve the public, for a change. He'd look for potential recruits among the cops if his own army wasn't shrinking daily. One recruit he would like was Mike Boucher, the Naskapi brave enough to mutiny against his RCMP bosses. Boucher had helped organize successful indigenous and settler resistance to RCMP schemes in British Columbia. Brave soldier, that one.

Chilliwack was helping with the rice works and Fraser Valley land reclamation for agriculture. Valcartier was helping Hydro Quebec, now an anarcho-syndicalist agency of real, progressive change. Cornwallis and Petawawa were in reclamation of lands hurt by mining in Nova Scotia and Ontario. Even Cold Lake had found useful work: aerial mapping as part of a Boreal Forest research project aimed at revitalizing those "lungs of the Earth," and reclamation of the tarsands sites, a big job indeed.

The army served the people and the land, and Helting was happy to help. He was also happy to answer to his region, not to distant Ottawa, and surely not to the North Atlantic Treaty Organization, that "stinking corpse of the Cold War" now finally dead and buried. What had been Alberta were now six regions, and Swift Fox Region was Wainwright's. The regional government in Medicine Hat was closer, more efficient, and more trusting than distant Ottawa had been. Helting liked being trusted. Being trusted made people more trustworthy, he figured. Medicine Hat assured him that good work in Haiti would bring postings in many other places ravaged by Canadian capitalism: Congo, Guatemala, Chile, Aceh.

"The president will see you now," a White House clerk told Bruce Culloden on a brisk spring morning. Washington had invited Culloden to help coordinate Canadian and USian laws regarding land use and indigenous sovereignty. He was sure that President Winona McKay, basking in an overwhelming election victory the previous fall, would have been briefed about him, a humble Canadian lawyer with Scottish roots. He had read much about her, the coal-haired muse who "smashed the war machine and fed the people," as the old slogan went.

"Welcome, Bruce," McKay said. "I'm so glad you could come."

"I'm very flattered that you invited me, Madame President."

"Call me Winona. You and I have much in common, more than you might think. May I call you Bruce?"

"By all means."

Culloden's quick brain scanned his history and McKay's, trying to anticipate her meaning. A lawyer who predicts better succeeds more often. Bruce's recent successes in Nemiah, the Chilcotin, and distant parts of Canada implied that his predictive powers worked well.

"Your background is Scottish, I believe," Winona said. "Mine is as well. Your name is the same as the site of a famous Scottish battle, a defeat for Scottish feudalism, but the seeds of modern Scottish independence from England."

"I'm sure that you know of the Highland Clearances, Bruce."

"Yes, my ancestors were among the people thrown off their land."

"You might like to know that my ancestors lost their land in the Clearances, too. I've been thinking about that lately, about the importance of land. How do you view land?"

"I don't go as far as Henry George and say that land is the source of all wealth, and should be the only thing taxed; but I do agree with many of the indigenous people with whom I've worked. They say, "It's all about the land. It has always been all about the land.""

"I agree, Bruce. I think we'll get on fine. I know that Canada's recent constitutional conference restored indigenous sovereignty over land. That was a brave act. I understand that the indigenous people of Canada have reciprocated by inviting settlers to share that land."

"You're well informed, Winona. That sharing of land was what the indigenous people who signed treaties centuries ago thought the treaties meant. Now there are no treaties, but that original impression has become the law of the land."

"It's all about the land," as you say. "I'm sure our Scottish ancestors said similar things, but in Gaelic."

"Well, Bruce, I have a nest of legal eagles waiting for you and whatever help you brought from Canada. The United States, that is, what's left of it, much of the Southwest and Southern California having rejoined Mexico, West Coast Communes now independent but friendly, Vermont, Maine, and some northern parts now part of Canada, and Alaska having declared independence; what's left of my country seeks guidance from your country in many areas. The one that made me invite you here is land law."

"I would be delighted to help. I have studied your law more than many Canadian lawyers do: I advocated for various indigenous groups in various United States courts."

"I know. That's one of many reasons that I think you are the person for the job. This is a big job, Bruce. I hope you brought help."

"You will be please to know, Winona, that the help I brought is at least as enthusiastic as I am to be part of this historic coordination. I brought young lawyers, even a few law students, old lawyers, indigenous lawyers, even a geographer and a hydrologist."

"Law, land, and water," President McKay observed. "I like it."

"I thought you would."

As Bruce Culloden walked the corridors of this former imperial power to huddle with his rangy team waiting in a cafeteria, he was relieved, albeit dubiously, that the new Canadian government, comprised of representatives of the 49 regions, had preserved the Office of the Prime Minister. Prime Minister Knight was surprisingly adept at the transition challenges, and a known figure on the world stage. Canada needed a presence on the world stage. It had much to offer the world. "Preserve" was the right word: preserving some antique institution until something more modern and democratic, arose to replace it. Perhaps the office would house a person nominated from among the 49, following traditional British parliamentary practice. Perhaps it would be a revolving committee from among the delegates. Perhaps society would evolve beyond the need for government, Bruce's cherished hope, now more likely to happen than any time since Napoleon and other European despots invented the nation state as a stick with which one class beat another.

———

"That's quite a garden you're planning, Randy," Holly said, the warm spring sun glinting on her raven-black hair. "Need help?"

"You got it. You're the right woman at the right time. Grab a shovel and follow me."

Right woman and right man, each person silently hoped at the same time.

Sarah sat in her rocker on the deck of the house, and watched the pair work. The winter had been hard on Sarah. Winter is hard on old people. The community gathering for her 94th birthday party a week ago had worn her down a bit more. She hadn't had to lift a finger, but it had taken energy merely to bask in the admiring gaze of the Nemiah people, and of people from far and wide. Celebrity is a burden, Sarah thought, as she rocked in the midday sun. Nice day to relax and watch others work.

"Did you notice the moon last night, Holly?" Sarah asked as Holly sweated into activity.

"Yes, I noticed the moon, Sarah," Holly said, without the irritation the question had once caused her. "Moonlight brings people together."

"Smart girl," Sarah winked. "You listening, Randy?"

"Yes, Granny."

———

"It's good to relax away from all those numbers, eh?" Mike Vidic said to Jennifer Brant, as they biked along the Williams Lake River Trail toward the Fraser River.

"Sure is, Mike," Jennifer said. "I'm surprised how clever some of these ex-bank employees are. I almost don't need to tell them what to do anymore."

"That's the sign of a good manager, Jen," Mike said. "The place operates well without you having to run around fixing people's messes."

"Does that mean that the less I do, the better manager I am? So I'm a genius if I do nothing at all?"

"You know that the important, hard work is setting up the system to run well, putting the right people in the right jobs and training them well. That's so much work that you deserve a break today."

"Isn't that the old MacDonald's hamburger slogan? Some days I miss those golden arches, but the worker co-op that took over MacDonald's a couple months ago makes a mean burger. Too bad it won't last."

"Is the co-op in trouble already?" Mike asked.

"The co-op is fine, but the burger is 'a shining artifact of the past,' as the song goes. As meat rises in cost to reflect the environmental harm entailed in its production, the hamburger will become as rare as a stock trader."

"I guess. No loss there," Mike said. "North Americans eat far too much meat, my mom and dad always said. Speaking of stocks, did you see the news story about the stock market museum? Clever idea, eh?"

The New York Stock Exchange had been cold with inactivity since the last crash finished it, and freed the world from the moneychangers. Their temple was being converted into a museum that included exhibits explaining how this casino base of capitalism had worked. Drumheller had the Tyrell Museum of Paleontology of dinosaur exhibits and other extinct curiosities. Why not a museum to display the extinct curiosities of stocks, bonds, puts, calls, margins, derivatives, futures, hedge funds, and frenetic activity from a greedy bygone era.

"Yes, I saw the story. Did you notice what the new plaque said at the main entrance? It was a quote from Adam Smith, the 1700s Scottish philosopher whose book <u>The Wealth of Nations</u> warned against joint stock companies and elucidated the labor theory of value. It was nice that it was made gender-neutral for the plaque: 'People of business cannot get together but that it ends in a conspiracy against the public good.'"

"Wanna conspire on the Fraser River bank after our picnic, Jennifer?" Mike asked, as they crossed the last bridges before the trail's end at the river.

"Would it be for the public good?" Jennifer asked slyly.

"You bad banker, you!"

"How's the young architect doing in Vancouver, Walter?" Kathy asked as Walter brought her tea.

"He'll be back tomorrow night and you can ask him yourself, Kathy," Walter replied. "But I'm happy to offer a sneak preview before the feast we plan to welcome back him and Maria."

"Maria?" Albert said from across the room.

"Maria is Leon's friend. They went to Vancouver together in Johanna's car," Kathy explained.

"Oh, that Maria!" Albert said. "I met her at the roadblock. Interesting blondie. Then she wintered in Nemiah until Christmas. She fit in well, like her parents. Good kid. Knows how to work."

"She and Leon worked together on the Richmond rice project and some land reclamation for agriculture in the Fraser Valley. She wants to study agriculture, in Guelph, I think," Rosalee said, having walked in during the conversation.

"One thing they might try to reclaim some Fraser Valley land for farming is The Oolichan Project, Chris was telling me when they came here last winter. It's named after the oily fish that people used to heat in barrels on the Pacific Coast, to extract the grease. A group of people who worked at the Alberta tarsands want to heat the asphalt and extract oil," Walter began.

There was irony in former tarsands workers naming their project after the fish whose grease lubricated trade along the Grease Trail in Central British Columbia. That trail, now a heritage trail full of eco-tourist activity, was not far south of the route of the proposed Northern Gateway Pipeline, which would have taken tarsand "bitumen" from Alberta to Pacific tidewater for export by tanker. Pipeline ruptures and the resulting lawsuits in Canada and elsewhere, and firm opposition to this recipe for ecological disaster, not only stopped the pipeline plan, but bankrupted Enbridge and almost all other pipeline companies.

"Chris and Maria think The Oolichan Project will be too energy intensive," Rosalee said. "She wants to dismantle roads to and uses the pavement to build terraced gardens on the surrounding slopes, and fence smallholdings for cooperative farmers."

Many Bengalis agreed with Maria, and gave her the wisdom of experience. They reminded her that collective farms work best when individual farmers have some control of the land they farm. There would be no kulaks, the bane of Soviet agriculture; but there would be no coercion forcing proud, productive farmers to become pliant, indifferent wage slaves.

The two projects were running side-by-side, to see which project uses energy better and gives more positive results. Chris and Maria predict that her project will become the preferred model, because the Oolichan Project won't be able to produce cost-competitive oil, given the sharply rising taxes and increasing regulation that fossil fuels face.

Oil finally had to pay its way environmentally. It didn't stand a chance against more benign energy sources, and conservation, each finally receiving public subsidy equivalent to what fossil fuels had long enjoyed.

The Fraser Valley land was beginning to breathe again, as people removed vast areas of pavement in parking lots and on highways. The fertile land below was free, as were the people who now controlled it.

Kathy asked, "You met Maria, then, eh, Rosalee? How do you like her for Chris?"

"I met her at the roadblock, but I talked to her more when she and Chris came from Vancouver in February to visit. She stayed overnight, on the hide-a-bed, then continued to Nemiah. Three days later, she was back, picked up Chris, and they returned to Richmond. They had come to bring her mom back to Nemiah. Johanna had sold the house to a co-op that would make it the headquarters for the expansion of that children's charity Johanna founded. A board comprised of people from the cultures whose children the charity serves will oversee the charity, now a worker co-op."

Lost and Found Innocents, Johanna van der Waals charity, was expanding, but in happier directions than it could have expanded. Some children traumatized by war still came to the funky building in East Vancouver, but the Vancouver Commune had delegated to the charity the child services formerly run, badly, by the province and the city. Johanna was confident that the charity staff, now its owners, and the board of directors, would handle the expansion well. They would hire the best and brightest from the dissolved government authorities.

"I remember reading about that charity," Kathy said. "I'd never heard of it during my years barricaded in the provincial government human services empire."

"That's a good description of that ministry, Kathy," Albert said. "It never did much good for us Indians. I'm glad it's gone. Mary Gaston runs a more approachable, more accountable operation in Williams Lake. She was wise to hire you ."

"Albert, you're such a flatterer. Stop it, or you might make me full of myself," Kathy blushed.

"When we get home, I'd happily make you full of something," Albert smirked.

"Albert!" Rosalee exclaimed.

"The Chilcotin man, like the busy beaver, just keeps on going," Walter chimed in.

"Don't you start, Walter. You have an early day tomorrow," Rosalee chided.

"Thanks for coming to my rescue, Rosalee," Kathy said. "I feel safe around you."

"That's because these two oafs respect their matriarchal Chilcotin culture, Kathy. They listen to me, or they face my nephews."

"Just kidding, Kathy," Albert said. "I don't want a pet. I want an equal."

"I know. That's why I haven't skinned you yet and sold your pelt, my beavering buddy."

Back across the river, the land was again under Chilcotin rule, a long-delayed correction of a historic wrong. As the Cariboo Shuswaps and Carrier did, the

Chilcotins accepted settler co-management of that land, for the good of all flora and fauna, and people, on it. River basin committees, comprised of representatives of all regions that a watershed touched, protected water, the giver of life, the guarantor of identity.

The people, those not corrupted by colonialism, those not bought nor sold, had always known who they were. Many settlers, their own identity too firm to heed the siren calls of racism or its many demonic cultural offspring such as pioneer literature hiding land theft, education hiding history, and money hiding morality, were happier now than before The Red Path had pierced and pulverized the whole rotten system. Identities mingled, like the Thompson and Fraser Rivers mingled at Lytton. Two powerful streams were becoming one, carrying memories, healing waters flowing toward a sea of possibilities.

Ten Years Later

"Look, Holly! An eagle!" Randy exclaimed, as they approached Sarah David's grave. "It's as if Sarah's spirit is telling us that everything will be all right."

Holly said, "And it's circling, Randy. Life is like a circle. Sometimes we go around and don't notice what beauty there is, in people, in nature, in eagles, in memories of special old women. Your granny was a special woman, Randy."

"I know it. So are you. I finally know that, after we circled each other for decades."

"Perhaps we were nervous. We were under colonial occupation, after all. Our masters, some of them our own people, set us against one another. For so long, we dared not trust one another. Divide and rule. A few years of freedom have done wonders, here, elsewhere, in people, in me."

"Do you trust me, Holly?" Randy asked.

"I do. I hope you trust me, Randy."

"I do."

These words, pronounced under an autumn afternoon sky of moving clouds and warming sun; these words, pronounced near a lake, under a tree exploding with yellow and orange leaves, reaffirmed the death of one way of life and the birth of another.

As dead leaves fall to the ground, and a tree stands dormant against winter blasts, settler colonialism had killed a way of life; but its people, the Chilcotin people, firmly rooted against generations of the icy blasts of miners, Indian agents, police, priests, teachers, industrialists, and an army of colonial conspirators intent on keeping them down, had come back, like new leaves sprouted on old trees.

Holly Daniels and Randy David joined hands and walked away from the grave of Sarah David, and along Konni Lake, their water, on their land.

Fifty Years Later

A couple generations had grown up in the new society, knowingly dependant on an environment healed much of the harm of centuries of destructive industrial activity and generations of debilitating population growth. The original revolutionaries were long dead, not eaten by the revolution, contrary to the French expression; but peacefully expired after long, productive lives. There were few monuments to them: this revolution produced a culture of progress, not a cult of personality. That progress was not the one-dimensional progress of economic growth, a measure so irrelevant that society had stopped measuring it soon after the revolution. Zero-growth economics meant a steady, sustainable environment and society. The free good had largely replaced the fiercely-fought-for good.

True progress is progress in the ability to make and enjoy a just world. People around the world had that ability. To the young, it seemed that this ethic, the only ethic they had known, was the only possible organizing principle of society, of the world. Cultural evolution had ascended from "nature, red in tooth and claw," to "nature, part of us, us part of it."

One result that pleased demographic theorists and put less strain on the environment was the population decline. So content had people become that their fertility rate plummeted. Unjust societies produce many children: people try to grow enough descendants to care for them as they age, in a society that cares not for them, old or young. Social supports were so strong now that people had nigh stopped having children, for decades. The world population had fallen below seven billion, then below six billion, and now it hovered just above five billion, still falling.

The four horsemen of the apocalypse, war, famine, plague, and death had not reduced the population. Instead, the birth rate had fallen far below replacement level, about 2.1 children per woman of child-bearing age. It was under 1.0 in most of the world, and lower in populous places. Freedom and security in society eliminated much of people's desire to seek freedom and security by having children. The death rate was little changed, but deaths so outnumbered births that population fell. As it fell, living standards rose for the remaining population.

Canada's population, by contrast, had risen to 79 million, no longer huddled in border-hugging cities, but spread evenly throughout a country challenged by global warming. That challenge had brought millions of climate warming refugees from the former United States and other warmer places. The former US, now a loose federation like Canada, had 141 million people on land that had held more than 200 million after several states had separated during the start of the world revolution.

China, for decades leading the world revolution, had 700 million people, a bit more than half its number fifty years earlier. This was due partly to out-migration, but due mostly to lower fertility. The "One Child Policy" of the 20th century had left the country with tens of millions more men than women, because people aborted girl babies as they tried for boy babies, in a sexist culture that was now sexist no more. Community, and material security for all, had dramatically reduced the fertility rate, now hovering just below 0.8.

The power of twins, of any sex, strong in Chilcotin tradition, continued, however; but children were seen as citizens of the world, not as commodities of the clan. Twin girls, born to Chris and Maria about 40 years earlier, now continued their aging parents' revolutionary traditions. Rosa and Johanna had grown up knowing that a revolution is a permanent fixture of society, not a brief, brilliant moment between two static states.

Johanna, dark like her dad, painted. Rosa, blonde like her mom, wrote. Each did her quota of public labor, which averaged about 20 hours per week throughout society, throughout the world. The rest of people's time was their own, although many continued working for better communities, and therefore a better world.

For example, a few years earlier, Johanna had served as the North of Lakes Region's representative in the federal parliament. She had moved there to seek inspiration from an area made famous by the Group of Seven, early-20th century painters of starkly beautiful trees and lakes. They had drunk from the streams, before industry had polluted them. When Johanna knelt by their crystalline waters, the streams were again clean enough for drinking.

Johanna had even been prime minister, a one-year appointment that rotated among the 57 regions that now comprised what had been Canada. The federal office was more titular than powerful, but it did inform Johanna about the world, and the world about Johanna's region and federation. With air travel long extinct, she had spent half the year touring the world, by boat and train mostly. Bicycling through Palestine, a world model of intercultural harmony, had been a highlight.

Her late grandmothers, Johanna and Rosa, would have been happy for her, happy they had joined millions who dared to make a new and better world.

Twins, Rosa and Johanna, living symbols of the unity that had come to a divided world.

The End

About the author

Michael Wynne was born and raised in a rural area west of Edmonton, Canada. This is his first novel. He had the idea of a socialist utopia novel for years, but learning of the National Novel Writing Month made him produce the novel, with various polemical and romantic asides whose composition surprised him. Of more than 300 000 who entered the worldwide event, Wynne was among the more than 41 000 who met the November 30, 2013 deadline of 50 000 words. Writing was fun and easier than he expected, but editing and formatting were harder. His quaint mind might grow a deep ecology novel next.

Made in the USA
San Bernardino, CA
05 July 2014